# TRANSACTIONAL LOVE: A STORY OF SURVIVAL AND PERSEVERANCE

BY: SARA MOUSA

# CONTENTS

# PREFACE

*"Love that demands a price is not love—it is a lesson in survival. But within the deepest wounds lies the greatest power to heal, to rise, and to love freely beyond all conditions."*

Love is often portrayed as pure, unconditional, and effortless—a force that lifts us up and connects us deeply to others. But what happens when love feels like a transaction, a delicate exchange where worth is measured by what we give or receive? For many of us, love is not always gentle. It can be entangled with survival, manipulation, and the desperate hope to be seen and valued.

*Transactional Love* is my story—a journey through the shadows of conditional affection, emotional survival, and the struggle to reclaim my sense of self. Raised in a world where love was often a currency tied to approval and control, I learned early on how to navigate emotional minefields and mask my true feelings to stay safe. Later, even in marriage, I found myself caught in familiar patterns that echoed childhood wounds.

But this is also a story of awakening and perseverance. It is about peeling back layers of pain to discover hidden strengths, uncovering rare gifts as a dark Heyoka empath, and embracing a cosmic identity as a starseed. It is about transforming survival into empowerment, learning to love authentically, and breaking free from cycles that once felt unbreakable.

Through these pages, I invite you to walk alongside me—not just to witness my story, but to find echoes of your own struggles and hopes. Whether you have faced conditional love, emotional manipulation, or the challenge of healing from deep wounds, this book is a testament to the resilience of the human spirit and the possibility of true transformation.

Welcome to *Transactional Love*. May it inspire you to survive, persevere, and ultimately, to thrive.

# INTRODUCTION

Love is often described as the most beautiful and natural of human experiences—a source of joy, comfort, and connection. Yet, for many, love feels complicated, conditional, and fraught with unspoken expectations. When love becomes transactional, it shifts from a free-flowing gift to a calculated exchange, where affection, approval, and worth are measured like currency.

This book is a raw and honest exploration of what it means to live and love under those conditions. It is a story of survival—navigating relationships marked by emotional manipulation, control, and the relentless pursuit of validation. It is also a story of perseverance, of breaking free from toxic cycles and learning to reclaim one's own identity and power.

Throughout my journey—from a childhood shaped by narcissistic dynamics to a marriage shadowed by the same patterns—I struggled to understand why love felt so elusive and conditional. But through spiritual healing and deep self-discovery, I uncovered not only the wounds but also the rare gifts within me: a dark Heyoka empath's ability to reflect truth and a starseed's cosmic calling to heal and transform.

*Transactional Love* is more than my story—it is a mirror for anyone who has felt trapped in the push and pull of conditional love, a guide for those seeking healing, and a testament to the resilience of the human spirit. Together, we will explore the patterns that bind us, the truths that set us free, and the possibility of love that transcends survival—a love rooted in authenticity, empathy, and radical self-acceptance.

Welcome to this journey. Your story matters, and your healing is possible.

Love is not always gentle.
Sometimes it's a quiet bargain,
a whispered trade of hope and pain—
a currency of hearts measured in scars.

In the shadows of conditional love,
where approval must be earned,
and affection weighs heavy like a debt,
survival becomes the language of the soul.

This is a story woven from those shadows—
of a child who learned to hide her truth,
of a woman who danced with ghosts of control and longing,
of a spirit awakening to a deeper power.

Through the storm of broken promises and silent wars,
I found a spark—an ember of resilience,
a dark mirror reflecting both pain and strength,
a cosmic call to heal beyond the earthly binds.

*Transactional Love* is a journey through that fire,
a testament to the fierce grace of perseverance,
and an invitation to embrace love that is wild,
free, and utterly true.

Step softly,
for this is a story of survival—
and the awakening of the heart.

"In innocence lies the quiet magic of beginnings—the pure soil where dreams first take root and hope blooms without fear."

# CHAPTER 1:
# INNOCENSE AND BEGINNINGS

Survival is not just about breathing, it's about rising—again and again—when the weight of the world seems too heavy to carry. I learned to navigate the chaos of narcissism, the silence of people-pleasing, and the isolation of single motherhood. But it was in the darkest moments that I found my true strength, and every step forward was a victory in a story that's still being written.

Life has a way of testing us, sometimes breaking us into pieces we didn't know could fit back together. I grew up in a house where love was conditional and affection was a game of manipulation. A mother who constantly gave to others and never to herself, and a father who twisted every word and every action into a means to control. From an early age, I was taught to please, to bend, to adapt to everyone else's needs, leaving my own buried in the noise. At 19, with a newborn baby and later having two other children, I became a mother not just by birth, but by the sheer will to survive. Raising them alone, I learned that survival wasn't about holding on—it was about letting go of the past and finding the strength to stand up, again and again, in the face of every storm. This is the story of how I learned to take my life back. How, against every odds, I chose to fight, to rise, and to live a life of my own making.

I was born in Abu Dhabi to Egyptian Muslim parents, both of whom were deeply rooted in the traditions of their homeland. From a young age, I was always quiet, a child who preferred the comfort of solitude over the chaos of social gatherings. I had no interest in mingling with the endless stream of family friends who filled our home—whether it was for a birthday party or just an afternoon of socializing. I would refuse to go greet them, retreating into my own little world. I was a highly observant child, watching the adults around me with a growing sense of confusion. It was as if I could see behind the curtain of this elaborate facade—everyone seemed to be playing pretend. The family I was supposed to belong to didn't feel real to me. There was a constant pressure to be more outgoing, to fit in with the noise and the forced smiles, but I never wanted to. I didn't want to be a part of this "happy family" persona that felt so far from the truth. I simply longed to be left alone, to make sense of a world that never quite felt like mine.

Growing up, my father would often tell me how much he appreciated how easy I was as a child, compliant, quiet, and never demanding anything. Unlike my two older sisters, who he would complain were loud and difficult, I was the one who never threw tantrums or asked for treats. He loved telling the story of how I would quietly walk beside him, hand in hand, as he ran errands, never asking for anything, and always declining any offers of sweets or rewards. At the time, I took pride in this, thinking it was just a part of who I was. But as an adult, after years of healing from the trauma of my childhood, I finally understood the truth. I wasn't being easy or calm because it was in my nature, I was simply trying to protect myself from the wrath of his anger. I had learned early on that the safest way to avoid conflict was to stay small, silent, and invisible. That quiet, complacent little girl wasn't showing restraint; she was afraid. I never felt safe enough to be my true self, to have needs, emotions, or desires of my own. I felt like I existed only to serve the wants and expectations of my parents and sisters, molding myself to fit the image they had of me. In their eyes, I wasn't a person, but a tool to carry out their vision for the future— a scapegoat, trapped in a role I never chose.

My father was the epitome of the proud, ego-driven Arab man, steeped in tradition and self-reliance. Born and raised in Egypt to a father who worked as a tailor and a stay-at-home mother, he was the middle child with an older brother and a younger sister. From a young age, he was burdened with a sense of responsibility that shaped his entire life. He often recounted a story from his childhood he held onto for years, one that seemed to have a profound impact on his view of trust. When he was just six years old, his mother had sent him downstairs to ask a neighbor for change for an Egyptian pound, with strict instructions to come back immediately, regardless of the outcome. Wanting to please her, he went to the neighbor, but when he was told there was no change, he took it upon himself to visit a nearby street vendor. There, a man approached him and, after hearing the boy's plight, offered to help by taking the money and crossing the street to get the change. At first, my father was pleased, feeling hopeful, but his optimism turned to disappointment when the man disappeared and never returned. Alone and heartbroken, my father had to return home and explain to his mother what happened, knowing full well that she would be upset with him for not following her instructions. This incident left a lasting scar on him, embedding a deep lesson about trust. From that moment on, he vowed to never trust anyone but himself, a sentiment that he carried with him throughout his life.

My father often spoke of his own father—strict, yet loving—who held firm expectations for his family, believing that providing for them was enough to justify his actions, no matter the cost. He recalled how his father insisted that everyone be at the dinner table together —no exceptions. His father made sure the family had everything they needed and took pride in being the provider, but what he never realized was that in doing so, he demanded the complete suppression of any discomfort or emotional response from his children. The cost of his father's "good provider" persona was the loss of any space to question his actions or express personal needs. One of the most striking stories my father shared was about how his father secretly married a younger woman behind his mother's back. When this betrayal came to light, his father expected the family to simply accept it, swallow their hurt, and allow him to continue as if nothing had changed. The message was clear: as long as he fulfilled his role as the man of the house—providing for the family—his actions were beyond reproach. No one was allowed to criticize or hold him accountable for how his choices impacted the family. His dominance over the family narrative was unquestionable, simply because he had fulfilled his duties as a provider, and that, in his eyes, made him exempt from the consequences of his behavior.

As I reflect on my father's influence, I can't help but think about my mother and the stark contrast in how she was shaped by her upbringing. My mother grew up as one of ten children, and the loss of her father at the tender age of twelve left her mother, my grandmother, as her unwavering source of strength. My grandmother was a woman of deep devotion, her home was always open to anyone in need, whether it was food, water, or companionship. Her capacity to help others was boundless, and she cared for her ten children with love and resilience that seemed beyond human limits. The boys in the family took over the responsibility of providing, while the girls were raised to cook, clean, and manage all the domestic tasks. Their family owned a small chicken shop that allowed them to put food on the table without struggle. At first, I admired my grandmother's selflessness—how she cared for not only her children but anyone who needed a place to go, a meal to eat, or someone to talk to. To me, it seemed like the epitome of generosity. But as I dug deeper and reflected on my own experiences, I began to see a different side. I realized that my mother's people-pleasing tendencies likely stemmed from the very environment that taught her to abandon herself in favor of others. The level of self-neglect required to open your heart and home to both your own children and the entire community, without ever asking for anything in return, wasn't as noble as it seemed—it was a deep, unspoken form of self-betrayal. Helping others is undeniably a generous act, but at that scale, it felt more like an attempt to gain acceptance and avoid rejection. In my eyes, it was a reflection of my grandmother's own fear of being unloved, masked under the guise of kindness and care—something that, unknowingly, was passed down to my mother.

Growing up, I watched my mother serve our family without question, without complaint, and without a single moment of rest or consideration for her own needs, and it utterly confused me. Part of me marveled at how incredible it seemed to have a mother who was so devoted, so willing to give every ounce of herself without ever taking a break. Even when her body was on the verge of collapse, she would sit for just five minutes, then rise again, as if there were no off button. It felt as though she was allergic to rest or self-care as if those concepts didn't exist in her world. My father, a very demanding man, would constantly keep her on her toes with requests—"Make me tea, make me coffee, iron my shirt, go get this, go get that"—all without a single "please" or "thank you." My mother's response was automatic as if her sole purpose was to fulfill his every command. It was as if she was more a robot than a person, activated at my father's whim. This dynamic was mirrored in how others treated her. She might have believed that she was being cared for when someone simply said, "Happy Birthday," or gave her a gift, but these gestures always felt thoughtless, more a reflection of the bare minimum than true appreciation. I remember the stark contrast when we celebrated my father's 70th birthday. Our family traveled from New Zealand to Melbourne, with all 15 of us making a three-hour road trip to Apollo Bay for a weeklong celebration—BBQs, music, family time, and excursions all dedicated to him. Yet, when it came to my mother's 70th, the contrast couldn't have been clearer. We briefly discussed going to Bali to celebrate her, but that conversation fizzled out, and nothing more came of it. There were no grand gestures, no celebration, not even a present. Life moved on, and somehow, my mother's needs were forgotten, just another silent sacrifice in a long line of unacknowledged efforts.

Watching the dynamics between my mother and father, I learned a painful lesson—that I, too, was not a person in my own right, but merely an extension of their needs. I was meant to be like my mother, a robot of sorts, existing solely to serve the demands and desires of a man. I was not allowed to have emotions, wants, or needs of my own. Whenever I dared to express anything, it was met with anger and rage from my father. How dare I want to be a person? How dare I have feelings? How dare I speak unless spoken to? I was nothing more than an object, created to serve and stay silent. Looking back at my childhood as an adult, I finally understand why I was always quiet, reserved, and preferred to be alone. I never asked for anything because I had been programmed to believe that I wasn't entitled to anything. But on a deeper level, it was also a survival mechanism—I knew that if I expressed a need or desire, it would be used against me. Love, in my house, was transactional: "I gave you what you wanted, now you must give me the peace, happiness, and love I demand." It wasn't mutual, it wasn't unconditional. I had always wanted to be peaceful, loving, and happy, and I gave those qualities to others freely, hoping to receive the same in return. But now I realize that my peace, happiness, and love were brought through material things—items or money given to me by my family as compensation for the lightness and joy I brought into their dark, transactional world.

Quite recently, I realized just how much I had been living as the robot I was programmed to be. Every weekend, without fail, I would visit my parents or my sister's house, whether I actually enjoyed being there or not. I would suffer in silence, thinking, "It's family, this is what you do," but deep down, I knew it wasn't fulfilling. So, I decided to experiment—when my mother had to travel back to New Zealand, I stopped showing up. I stopped going to a place where I didn't feel loved or accepted but merely tolerated. For six weeks straight, my mother called every weekend, asking if I had visited my sister. I would tell her no, I was busy, and she would try to guilt-trip me into going, saying things like, "Why won't you go? This is your sister; she always helps you financially and with material things when you need it." What struck me the most was that during those six weeks, not once did my sister reach out to me to ask why I hadn't been over or invited me. That was when it hit me, my mother didn't care whether I was there or not; she was just desperately holding onto the delusion of a happy family that she had curated and maintained for years. My absence, my disconnection, threatened the image she worked so hard to build. The family was a sham, a fake attempt to present an image of superiority to friends and extended family as if ours was the perfect, functional family while others had fallen apart. For the longest time, I couldn't understand why I was the one held accountable for my choices while everyone else seemed to get a pass. Why wasn't my mother calling my sister to ask why she wasn't making an effort to spend time with me? Our family was unraveling, and all my mother could say was, "I miss the old you, I want her back." It was at that moment that I finally understood: she didn't miss me, she missed the version of me that complied with her idea of a family, the version of me that kept her illusion intact.

"The hidden third child carries the unspoken stories—living between shadows and light, unseen yet deeply felt, holding the keys to family secrets and silent strength."

# CHAPTER 2:
# THE HIDDEN THIRD

Being the third-born daughter in a family of three girls often felt like I was a footnote in a story that was already written. My older sisters were the ones who paved the way, setting the tone for what it meant to be seen and heard. I was the quiet one, the observer, always standing just outside the spotlight that they seemed to naturally step into. There were moments when I felt like the last piece in a puzzle that didn't quite fit, but in my silence, I learned to navigate the spaces between them. The oldest was the leader, the first to break the rules and take the blame. The middle one was the dreamer, full of fire and always creating a stir. And then there was me—the one who tried not to make waves tried not to ask for too much and ended up blending into the background. But it wasn't all bad. In the quiet, I learned resilience, and in the shadows, I discovered strength. Perhaps the third-born doesn't always get the applause, but in the quiet moments, we become the quiet force that keeps things moving forward.

I always felt like my eldest sister, just three years older, was a stranger in our house. She was quick to anger, emotional, and always stressed, often creating tension. While she fought for everything, my middle sister and I seemed to get things by default, which only added to the rift between us. She resented how easily I took what I wanted, while she overthought every decision. A key moment was when my dad offered her a brand-new iPhone, but she refused, saying it was a gift for him, and he should keep it or sell it. I took it immediately, when he offered it to me, no questions asked, which angered her. She felt I was being insensitive as it was a gift that he did not need nor want. I never understood her hesitation, and it angered her that I was so indifferent. We were polar opposites in that sense. She later told me how she disliked me for my rebellious behavior as a teen, feeling my parents blamed her for my actions as if she were responsible for keeping me in check and setting the example. But to me, she was just someone who lived in the same house, and we were never close—our relationship always felt distant, like we were strangers.

I believe my eldest sister is the most deeply affected and trauma-bonded to our parents more than the rest of us. As the firstborn, her connection to them runs deeper, and her role in the family dynamic is shaped by the responsibilities placed on her from an early age. Psychologically, first-born children are often independent, trailblazing, and more likely to take on a caretaker role, sometimes becoming surrogate parents for younger siblings. This partly explains why she felt responsible for my behavior as a teenager. Daughters of narcissistic fathers, like our own, often struggle with low self-esteem, perfectionism, people-pleasing, and emotional dysregulation, all of which I observed in my sister throughout our lives. Her challenges weren't just a result of our father's narcissism but also stemmed from our mother's insecurities and her own need to please. I now realize how damaging that was, especially when I reflect on how our mother, in a misguided attempt to "help," shamed my sister into losing weight, even singing a song to mock her that my middle sister and I were encouraged to sing along. It's something I didn't think much of at the time, but looking back, my mother played a significant role in causing the emotional damage. My eldest sister was often taken advantage of, and I remember one of her past partners commenting, "Are you going to the gym after eating that?" She even asked me once to take a pizza box home to hide it from her husband, so he wouldn't think she'd eaten it. To this day, it's hard for her to see our parents for who they really are and how their influence shaped our lives. She remains a self-confessed "daddy's girl," still unaware of the toxic, transactional love he offered us.

My eldest sister and I have always been estranged, and we rarely see eye to eye. Her constant attempts to project her misery onto me finally ended when I reached my breaking point and yelled at her to F**k off. It happened when she verbally attacked me for mentioning what I wanted as a gift for my birthday in our family chat, barely a week or two after a dear family friend had passed away from COVID. What she didn't know was that I had already told my middle sister and mother on the phone that I didn't want anything due to the recent loss, but they insisted, so I gave in. This wasn't the first time my sister tried to pick fights and stir drama, and until that moment, I had always listened to my mother's advice to ignore her and be the bigger person, saying "You know she's crazy." I let it slide repeatedly over the years, trying to keep the peace, thinking it was the right thing to do. What I didn't realize at the time was that I was keeping everyone else's peace but my own, and in doing so, I had adopted my mother's lack of boundaries as my own.

I always wondered why I never had a good, or even any, relationship with my oldest sister, and I've come to realize that I was robbed of this connection by my parents and their inability to foster healthy relationships. Everything was always about control and serving my father's needs as the "man of the house." Our family dynamic was often highly dysfunctional, with one or both parents behaving in hurtful ways towards each other and us girls.

Growing up in an environment filled with conflict, chaos, and a lack of protection profoundly impacted how we relate to each other as adults. I always felt like there was an unspoken competition between my oldest sister and me for our parents' attention. I saw this clearly when my middle sister was getting married. Our eldest sister expressed how jealous and annoyed she was that all the attention was focused on our middle sister. As an adult, I now understand that you can't expect people to foster something they never had or were incapable of maintaining themselves. We developed an "every man for himself" coping strategy. Parentification, a form of emotional abuse where a child is forced into the caretaker role for their parents and siblings, is something my eldest sister clearly experienced.

There are many reasons why as children we become disconnected from our siblings, particularly when we grow up in a dysfunctional family. Often, our parents overtly favor one child over another, setting up siblings to compete for attention and approval. In families such as ours where nurture is withheld from all children, as siblings we find ourselves vying for whatever scraps of affection our parents might offer. As children in these situations we often feel hurt, frustrated, and even rage toward our parents, but are too afraid to express these feelings directly. Out of fear of further abuse or worry that expressing any negativity will make us lose all chance of receiving positive attention. It's easier for us as children to take out our hurt on our siblings, as the stakes are lower. Instead of bonding over a shared painful experience, we end up venting our anger at each other, which can lead to a lifetime of hostility and estrangement. Sometimes, one sibling (me) might long to be close to the other, but the other may reject them, often out of jealousy. As siblings from a troubled home, we can mistakenly perceive that the other received more love, attention, and care, deepening the divide between us.

Growing up, I always felt a stronger connection with my middle sister than with my oldest. As kids, we spent a lot of time together—whether we were playing video games, joking around, or just talking. She always had this tough-girl persona, though I'm not sure if it was something she adopted or if it came from her high school reputation. Either way, I always felt safe and protected when she was around. In high school, she had two different Island girls try to start fights with her, but even though they were bigger, my sister handled them easily. That's when she earned her reputation as someone not to mess with. Being known as her little sister meant people knew not to mess with me either, or they'd have to deal with her. For most of my life, I felt proud and shielded by her. I even remember a time when I was about 11 or 12 and she kicked me while I was sitting on my bed, trying to eat a sandwich without making a mess. I ended up jolting the plate and cracked/broke my tooth. She immediately begged me not to tell Mom, and I could see the genuine fear in her eyes, so I didn't. I told Mum I was careless and blamed myself, and in that moment, I felt our bond had grown even stronger.

I never paid much attention to my middle sister's struggles growing up, mainly because my father and oldest sister were always at the center of attention with their constant drama and tension. But as I reflect now, I can see some of the challenges my sister faced. As a teenager, she dealt with weight issues and would grind her teeth at night. In her late teens and early 20s, she turned to alcohol, drinking and partying every weekend with her friends. One time, she asked me to help her clean her apartment in the city before moving to Melbourne from Auckland. When I walked in, I was taken aback by the stacks of empty liquor bottles lined up on the top shelf of her kitchen, almost like a proud display. At the time, we didn't think much of it—we were all young, trying to act cool, not realizing we were just numbing the pain we didn't realize we had. Alcohol was her vice, marijuana was mine, and as for my older sister... Well, who knows? We're all a bit like strangers in a lot of ways.

My middle sister went through a lot of loss at a young age. She lost her best friend, along with three other friends, in the same car accident. Another friend died after a fence post pierced her throat in a crash caused by getting into a car with a drunk driver. Then, another friend passed away after falling asleep at the wheel while driving home from work. These deaths happened within a two-year span, and it's clear that my sister really struggled with all the loss in such a short amount of time. I can't say for certain what impact this had on her, or if our upbringing affected her in the same way it did me since my family never really talks about emotions or personal experiences. Everything is kept quiet—"hush-hush." It's always "keep it to yourself" because no one has the time or energy to care about anyone else's problems. Growing up, I often felt completely alone.

It's safe to say that we were all left to fend for ourselves, struggling in silence, dealing with our issues alone, and isolating ourselves because no one had the capacity to handle anything. We were a family of strangers, suppressing emotions and facing challenges without support. There was no guidance, no love, no communication—just a silent expectation to "shut up and get on with it." Looking back, it's clear that I never learned how to ask for help. I had to toughen up quickly, grow up fast, and face major emotions, life events, and tough situations on my own—just like my sisters. How could we expect help or support when our parents couldn't even help themselves? It was a cycle of constant struggle, one thing after another. The message we got was that when it came to emotions and experiences, you had to rely on yourself, but if you needed money or material things, they'd be there for you. It was love, but transactional.

As we got older and my middle sister moved to Melbourne while I stayed in Auckland, our relationship grew more distant. I did visit her in Melbourne a few times, and during those visits, I continued to watch her struggle with alcohol and relationships. Although, when she met her now-husband, her life began to change. She slowly stopped drinking, their relationship developed, and eventually, they married and had four children. I believe that helped ground her and, in some ways, started to heal her. Still, I can't say for certain how these things affected her since we never talked about them—it's all just my perspective. I always thought my middle sister was the one person I could rely on in the family. She was there for me when I needed her, especially financially, or for advice on work or university assignments. I never hesitated to ask for help with those things, but when it came to emotions or major life events, I learned quickly that you're on your own.

As I began my own healing journey and started having realizations, I began to notice a side of my sister I hadn't seen before—little sly remarks she'd make that I hadn't paid much attention to, assuming she was just teasing or playfully bullying me. One time, I was visiting her, all dressed up with my hair and makeup done. I've always been someone who tries to hype myself up, saying things like, "Damn, I look good." That's when she asked me a question that really caught me off guard. She said, "Do you think if you stood next to a supermodel, a man would pick you over her?" My immediate response was, "I don't care about being picked by a man, I pick myself." She pushed further, saying, "Yeah, but if you couldn't pick yourself, I mean, seriously?" I asked, "Why not?" and she tried to brush it off as her just giving me a "reality check," implying I wasn't as attractive as I thought I was. At the time, I was delusional enough to believe that she loved me and would never hurt me, so hearing that comment was really painful. I immediately retreated to my room and isolated myself. Looking back now, I realize that her comment was more about her own insecurities than about me, but at the time, I couldn't help but feel hurt. It created more distance between us, and I also started to notice that her bond with my oldest sister grew stronger as they both lived in Melbourne—my middle sister for 10 years and my oldest for 5. I started to feel more and more excluded and pushed out of the family.

I always felt like the black sheep of the family, the outcast. I never seemed to fit into our family dynamic, and I couldn't relate to anyone. So, you can imagine how painful it was when the one person I thought I connected with on some level turned out to be a bit of a hater. One example of this happened when I finally moved to Melbourne, 10 years after she had. Once I settled in, got a job I liked, and was doing well, I took an opportunity at work to create a presentation on effective communication. If it was successful, it would be part of the company's onboarding process, and I'd be promoted to a higher position as a nurse educator. When I shared the good news with her, the first thing she said was, "What do you know about effective communication?" It was these little digs that kept driving a wedge between us, and I couldn't understand why she was acting this way until I took the time to reflect on my life. I realized that everything my family said or did to me was less about me and more about their own issues and insecurities. I was their punching bag, their outlet for releasing their pain. My light, my ability to keep going despite it all, really irritated their inner darkness because they were too caught up in their own lives to sit with themselves and reflect on their own issues. Instead, they chose to project their pain onto me.

"Quiet rebellion is the strength that whispers in silence—the gentle defiance that refuses to be broken, even when no one is watching."

# CHAPTER 3:
# THE QUIET REBELLION

Sometimes, the loudest rebellion is found in silence. It's in refusing to play a game you never agreed to, in standing apart without making a sound. During my pre-teen and teen years, I learned early that the quietest rebellion often went unnoticed. I didn't raise my voice or act out in loud ways, but inside, I was rebelling against everything I couldn't change. The family dynamics, the silence, the unspoken rules, I resisted them all by simply *not* conforming. I remember sitting at the dinner table, feeling like a ghost, while everyone else talked over me, assuming I was too quiet to have anything to say. But my silence wasn't surrender, it was my way of reclaiming a space that no one bothered to notice. While they carried on, I built walls in my mind, a quiet protest against a world that never took the time to ask, "How are you?" My rebellion wasn't loud; it was in the moments I chose not to play their game. The most powerful thing I did was refuse to be what they expected.

There were times when I'd say something, and no one would hear me, but then the person sitting closest would repeat what I said and suddenly get a positive response from the rest of the table. It made me wonder for a moment, why was I so invisible in my own family. Why did they only notice me when they wanted to take something from me and make it their own? This was just one of many examples. At other times, it felt like I only existed when they needed something: reassurance, a confidence boost, to hear that they were doing the right thing, or to get a compliment or service completed. It was as if I were on standby, waiting for someone to come to me whenever they needed something, otherwise, it didn't matter. I was the go-to person in my family because I'm a doer. I don't hesitate long before acting on something that piques my interest. I've always been a quiet observer and an information seeker. While the rest of my family focused on daily life, I was always contemplating the bigger questions, like the meaning of life itself.

Looking back at my childhood and how invisible I felt, I realized two things. First, I was conditioned to serve others and abandon my own needs. Affection was never given freely, I had to ask for it. I was always the one running errands for everyone, going to the store, picking up packages, finding the best deals, and searching for the services they needed to complete their tasks. It felt like I was assigned the role of a personal assistant to the entire family, but this was all hidden under the guise of "helping me" and masked by fear tactics and monetary payments as needed. They created this dependency on me while failing to realize they were the ones who fostered it. They kept me so preoccupied with fulfilling their needs that I didn't have the time or energy to pay attention to my own. I didn't even know what I needed or wanted because I never had the chance to figure it out.

The second realization was that the only time they truly saw me was when I did something that caused trouble and they had no choice but to deal with it. I remember when both my mother and sister had to go to the hospital for life-threatening surgeries. As someone who had been ignored my whole life, that period only highlighted my invisibility and pushed me to create behaviors that demanded attention. I was 14 at the time and got caught stealing from a department store. The police officer who brought me home turned to me and said, "You live in such a nice home, why would you steal?" I stayed silent, but in my mind, I thought it wasn't about the things, it was about the thrill of possibly being caught or, at least, being seen. From that perspective, the invisible child just wants to be noticed, "Hello, I exist!" Did it really have to come to this for me to get some attention? The deprivation was real.

My teenage years were a confusing and challenging time. I didn't really know who I was, and I often felt invisible, like a caged animal in my own home—only let out when someone needed something from me. Otherwise, I felt safer staying alone in my room. I quickly learned that expressing any needs or desires would only lead to anger, irritation, or just a flat "no." Even asking for something took so much courage, and hearing "no" was always hard to bear. Eventually, I decided, "Why bother?" and started doing whatever I wanted behind my parents' backs. A few times, I got caught, but it didn't really matter because I knew the consequences would never change anything. I'd just slip back into being invisible. I started hanging out with the wrong crowd, taking things that weren't mine, and sneaking out of my window at night to go to parties and clubs when I was 14. I was shocked by how little anyone cared about my age, they just saw a "hot girl with paying males" and let me in. I even used my sister's ID to get into clubs, and they barely looked at it. At 14, I had my first puppy-love boyfriend, tried smoking and liquor, and experimented with cannabis at 15. It was as if a switch flipped in me when I turned 14. Suddenly, a whole new world was there for the taking. I realized that my parents' parenting style was "out of sight, out of mind." Do whatever you want, just don't let me find out. I can now understand that this stemmed from their fears and lack of general attention to detail.

Ever heard the saying "the proof is in the pudding"? Well, how's anyone supposed to see the pudding if they never bother to pay attention? I always understood the assignment because I was the one watching the pudding closely. I could see where attention was lacking, and I made my moves around that. I noticed everything and was always three steps ahead. The only time I'd slip up was when I got too greedy or too impatient.

A good example of this was when I started dating my ex-husband (then boyfriend). Like any teenage girl, I wanted to spend time with him, so I came up with a plan to get what I wanted without causing any problems. At the time, I worked as a waitress at a restaurant, so I told the staff there that I'd lie to my mother and say I was going to work when I was really going to see my boyfriend. I asked them that if she ever called and I wasn't there, they should just tell her I was in the bathroom and would call her back. This plan worked perfectly. The pudding was clear when a jealous friend of mine, who was having a moment, called my mother and told her I wasn't at work but was with my boyfriend. She then called me immediately, upset, crying, and frantically apologizing.

But here's the thing: Right after I hung up, I got a call from my workplace letting me know that my mom had called and they told her I was in the bathroom. By that point, I was already halfway to work because my so-called friend had tipped me off about her betrayal. I got to work, called my mom back, reassured her that my friend had acted out, and confirmed I was, in fact, at work. Crisis averted. Always pay attention to the pudding!

As a quiet child and a subtly rebellious teenager, I always found joy in whatever I experienced, whether good or bad. I had a habit of looking at the bright side, the silver lining. Why? Because, even though I faced struggles and got really messed up at times, I understood that every situation has two sides. There's always a mix of good in the bad and bad in the good; it all depends on my perspective and which side I choose to focus on. I always chose to focus on the good. I also came to realize that the bad moments often came from the fact that I wasn't able to meet someone else's wants or needs. Others might have thought they had control over me, and to some extent, they did, but in my mind, I allowed it because I needed something from them. The experiences I had with people in my past helped shape who I am today. I used to firmly believe that a good heart with good intentions will always succeed. As I often would say, "If you do good things, good things happen; if you do bad things, bad things happen." This is the universal law of cause and effect, or karma, and I learned to live by it early on.

By the time I was 16, I had realized that if I could make people believe they had some level of control or authority over me, I could get them to do anything I wanted, willingly. I discovered that there was a hidden power in innocence and vulnerability, something no one around me seemed to understand. I had always been fascinated by human behavior, observing everything around me, and I mean *everything*. For example, when I had my first serious boyfriend at 15, a year-long relationship, I noticed how busy and distracted his mind often was. He was constantly focused on work or his friends, looking stressed and overwhelmed. I learned to use my vulnerability at the right moments to ask for things when he wasn't fully present. I found that he was often willing to give, not because I demanded it, but because I asked at a time when he was too tired or stressed to say no. At the time, I didn't realize this was what I was doing, it just came naturally to me.

I've always had an innocent appearance, both in how I looked and in my energy. I may have seemed naive, and in some ways, I was, but I was also very strategic, shaped by my keen observations. I acted from a place of sincerity and vision, never intending to harm anyone. However, I often found that I unintentionally triggered people. This happened because I was always truthful and saw things for what they were, which meant I couldn't be easily manipulated or deceived in a way that would hurt me. I chose my battles carefully and didn't accept behaviors from others that didn't align with my values. I did what I needed to do to survive, but never at the cost of someone else, as I firmly believed in karma and made sure not to invite any bad energy into my life.

While some of my experiences in my teen years and early 20s might suggest that I was easily emotionally manipulated, I realize now that it was more a result of being conditioned as a child to suppress my own feelings in order to prioritize others and their emotions. Yes, to some extent, I did this, but it wasn't so much about seeking approval as it was about trying to feel safe in my environment. It wasn't about passively accepting that I should just follow orders without questioning them, it was about finding a way to navigate my surroundings. Looking back, I see that, even though I was constantly told to be "the bigger person" while meeting everyone else's needs, I still stayed true to my own emotions and felt them deeply. This often got me labeled as "too sensitive," as if feeling deeply was a weakness. I quickly learned that no one really cared about how I felt because they were too focused on themselves. So, I kept my feelings to myself and taught myself to manage on my own.

I became a parent, not only to myself but also to those around me, both at home and outside of it. I did this in subtle ways, where I never made anyone feel inferior or less than. Instead, I encouraged them to take action in a way that felt like their own choice, as if I had no influence at all, just a gentle nudge in the right direction. I did this because I could sense the fragility of people's egos. I saw childlike behaviors in those around me, often feeling like I was dealing with overgrown toddlers, yelling, shouting, and throwing tantrums to get their way. They were constantly seeking validation from others, preaching "what will others think", while I had already validated myself and didn't need, nor want their approval. I was simply confused, trying to understand why things were this way.

My teen years went by quickly, and I had to mature fast. When I met my ex-husband, who was my boyfriend at the time, I was 16. He love-bombed me intensely, and I fell for him quickly. He gave me the attention and affection I had longed for from my family, especially from my father. My father had emotionally abandoned me long ago, focused only on his own comfort and control. He was always physically present in his home office, but emotionally absent in every other way. So, it was only natural that I would be drawn to someone who offered the love, care, and attention my father couldn't. After a year of feeling loved and special by this guy, he asked me to move in with him. Coming from a conservative Muslim family where nothing was ever openly discussed, I wasn't about to sit down and have that conversation with my parents. Instead, I simply agreed. At 17, head over heels in love and yearning for freedom, I packed up my things and snuck out of my window late at night. I wrote a long goodbye letter, especially expressing my deep resentment toward my father. My sister and mother found it first, quickly discarded it, and never showed it to my father in an effort to avoid making things worse. I didn't care; I just wanted to be honest and express my feelings, no matter how they felt about it.

"Marriage and children weave a visible life, but within the quiet corners lie hidden desires—silent sparks that shape who we are beyond what we show."

# CHAPTER 4:
# MARRIAGE, CHILDREN, AND HIDDEN DESIRES

At 18, I found myself at the crossroads of adulthood, getting married, with a child on the way. It was a whirlwind, a leap into something that, at the time, felt like both a privilege and a challenge. But beneath the excitement, there was a quiet determination inside me. I wasn't just trying to navigate the complexities of marriage and parenthood, I was trying to prove something.

I wanted to show my parents how it could be done differently. Growing up, love in our home felt distant, transactional, and controlled by unspoken rules and quiet absences. My father, always physically present, was emotionally a stranger, and my mother, though loving, often seemed overwhelmed, caught in a web of unspoken expectations. So, when I became a mother, I promised myself I would create a different reality for my own children, one full of warmth, nurturing, and genuine connection. I didn't just want to be a good parent; I wanted to be the kind of parent my parents couldn't be.

I poured all my energy into being loving, present, and caring, sometimes too much for my own good. It wasn't about perfection; it was about showing them that parenting could be an act of love, not obligation. I wanted my parents to see what it looked like to nurture a child not just with food or shelter, but with attention, affection, and time. Deep down, I thought if I did it right, they would finally see what I had always longed for, a real connection, one rooted in understanding and care.

My relationship with my ex-husband was an emotional roller coaster. At the time, I didn't know what narcissism was, so all I could do was observe his behavior, try to make sense of it, and navigate the constant ups and downs the best I could, all while keeping myself and my children safe. When I first met him, I was caught up in the whirlwind of love and chemistry, but being someone conditioned to neglect and suppress my own feelings in favor of catering to others, I became increasingly observant. I had to create a behavioral pattern, anticipating what needed to be done and what he desired, so I could manage everything quickly and avoid triggering his temper tantrums. At the time, I had no idea that moving in with him, after escaping the chaos of my own family, was just stepping into a different kind of hell.

Before I moved in with him and his family, I had noticed small signs of his anger, but nothing could have prepared me for what was to come. The first time I experienced any kind of violent attention from him was when I planned a day out to the mall with a girlfriend who was already on her way to pick me up. Naturally, I didn't think anything was wrong with this. But my boyfriend had a different perspective. When I told him about my plans, he exploded in anger, accusing me of thinking, "You can come and go as you please now that you live with me." In my mind, I thought, *yeah, I didn't realize I was just moving from one controlled environment to another.* I couldn't understand why I kept finding myself in situations where I was expected to surrender my independence in the name of love. That's when his true nature came out. He threw me across the hallway, and kicked me right in the face, splattering blood all over the walls as it dripped down my face. I screamed and cried, frantic and unsure of what to do. In desperation, I turned to his mother, who had come to see what the commotion was. But when I tried to express my distress, she quickly shut me down, yelling at me not to raise my voice at her. At that moment, she diverted all the attention to her own need to assert control, putting me back in my place without a second thought. I felt crazy not understanding why this was the response I was receiving. Why was I so hard to love? Unconditionally without control?

My friend, completely unaware of the chaos she was about to walk into, arrived with a smile that quickly faded. I was being thrown out for daring to make decisions for myself and wanting to do things any normal teenage girl would want to do. My boyfriend was throwing all my belongings outside, shouting at me to go live with my friend since I clearly wanted to be with her so badly. It was an overreaction, to say the least. My friend rushed to help me gather my things, tossing them into the trunk of her car, and we quickly drove off. She kindly let me stay with her and her mother until I could figure out my next move. I didn't want to go back to him, but I also didn't want to return to my family. I had to weigh my options carefully, deciding what would be the lesser of two evils.

Two days later, my boyfriend showed up at my university, asking to talk. He immediately started crying, apologizing, and professing his love for me. He told me how much he regretted what had happened and promised he would never do it again. The lesser of two evils now presented itself to me in the form of emotional manipulation. And it worked because once again, I was conditioned to put everyone else's needs and wants before my own.

I eventually moved back in with my boyfriend, now constantly on high alert. I figured that at least with him, I could carve out some semblance of freedom, as long as I observed his behavior carefully and navigated situations strategically. For the most part, I played along with his demands, doing what he wanted. During the times he wasn't around, either working or otherwise, I would focus on building myself up, educating myself, and searching for answers. I became obsessed with gathering information, observing his every move, analyzing situations, and devising strategies to minimize the impact of his behavior, all while trying to figure out a way to safely escape.

I spent 11 years with this man, enduring constant abuse, intimidation, and threats. The physical abuse was sporadic, only a handful of times, usually when he was intoxicated. One night, he woke me up, accusing me of stealing his cigarettes. I ended up with a black eye and a swollen lip after he threw my wallet at me, taking my money to buy new cigarettes. It wasn't until later that I learned it was actually his brother who had taken them.

These events took place before we got married when I was 18 and pregnant with our first child. I don't remember exactly how or when my family began to slowly reconnect with me during this time, but somehow, I ended up marrying this man in the internal affairs office, dressed in black and three months pregnant, with only our two mothers there. At the time, I felt pressured into it, mainly because of my family's religious and cultural expectations, and my mother's worry about what people would think. As for the wedding reception, it was held at the local food court, where we served butter chicken.

I naively thought that maybe now that we are married, my husband might change and feel more secure in our relationship since it is now official. Boy, was I wrong, what I learned from that situation is that it doesn't matter how much of the external world you try to change, it won't make a difference to his internal state. So, the abuse continued, now behind closed doors and on the hush-hush. I endured this torture for years because of my conditioning to abandon myself for the service of others. There was a breaking point to his physical abuse and that came around the time when my second child was born, I was 20 years old at the time. My children were 1 and 2 years old, they slept soundly next to me while my husband was out drinking. He returned home at around 2:30 am intoxicated and ready to create chaos. It started with him waking me up to initiate intimacy, which as you can imagine I was not into it. However, I felt obligated to do what he wanted to avoid his abuse and escalation of the situation as he was far beyond reason at this point. He noticed that I was not engaging and merely laying there for him to just do what he would to get it over and done with. It enraged him and the accusation that I wasn't into it because I had already done it with someone else started.

I thought oh no… this is it, he is going to kill me! I looked at his soulless eyes full of rage, anger, and hatred towards me. He grabs me by the hair and pulls me down to the ground, ready to beat the life out of me. I grab the pillow on the way down, place it over my face, and hold on for dear life. He kept pulling at my hair, trying with all his might to get that pillow off my face but by the will of god inside me, there was no way that pillow was coming off my face. He tried punching me through it as he pulled chunks of my hair out of my head until he just stopped. It was as if he came back to his senses and realized that if he kept going he was literally going to kill me and I could see that scared him a little. He left the room to calm down and I immediately had the courage to call the police and this was the first time I had ever done so. After that day, 5 years into our relationship, he never hit me again, but everything else continued.

I treated my husband like a rebellious teenager who refused to listen or change. It felt like I was always scolding or nagging him, but nothing I said ever seemed to reach him. Looking back, I now realize that the reason he didn't respond was because he never truly saw me as a person. He was so consumed by his own struggles and inner battles that he had no time, energy, or attention left for me. How could he, when his mind was constantly tangled in dark thoughts? I genuinely wanted to love him, to help him heal and grow, and I felt sympathy for the pain from his childhood. I thought I could ease his suffering, but in trying to carry his burdens, I was only dragging myself down into the darkness of his mind, instead of lifting him into the light of my heart.

Over the course of the 11 years we were together, I gradually stopped giving him the attention, love, and care I once did, and instead, focused all my energy on myself and my children. He became just a man with mental health issues that I coexisted with, waiting for the moment when I could finally escape. As time passed, the power dynamics shifted. He could see I no longer cared about his actions; the nagging stopped, my attention waned, and my focus was solely on improving myself, building my strength, and caring for my children. By the time my third child was born when I was 22, and seven years into our relationship, my husband was constantly getting into trouble, facing arrests for multiple DUI charges and accusations from his extended family. He ended up in prison when our third child was born, and while it was a difficult situation, it was, in a strange way, a blessing for me. It gave me a much-needed break from his toxic energy.

It wasn't until I was 27, in the final stretch of my first year working towards my Bachelor of Nursing degree, that God sent me an angel in disguise. It happened on the weekend before my final exams when my husband came home from a night of drinking with friends. Normally, I'm not the type to snoop, feel jealous, or keep tabs on his activities. I never had the time, energy, or attention to worry about what he was doing. I already knew he wasn't a great person, but my own conditioning kept me from fully acknowledging that and leaving much earlier. In the early hours of November 2015, my husband collapsed face-first onto the pillow and immediately passed out. Then, something inside me, a voice I can only call my intuition, urged me to look at his phone. I've always trusted my intuition, and when it speaks, I listen like my life depends on it. So, I picked up his phone and scrolled through his messages, nothing suspicious. I then checked his photo gallery, and there were some odd pictures from a trip to the beach, where it seemed like someone else had taken the photos. He had never mentioned going to the beach, but I figured I'd just ask him about it when he woke up. Just as I was about to put the phone down, that voice told me again, "Wait, look at the deleted images." I followed it and discovered several intimate photos of him with an unidentified woman, pictures of them cuddling, kissing, and holding each other in a way that was unmistakable.

I paused for a moment, trying to process what I had just seen. My blood was boiling, rage coursing through my body from my pinky toe all the way to the top of my head. After everything I had done for this man, after everything I'd endured, how could he go and find someone else? No offense to her, but let's be real, I look damn good, and yet he chose *that*? How dare he? The fury inside me built up like a tidal wave like I was winding up a fist to release every ounce of that rage. And then—bam—I slammed my fist into his back, knocking the wind out of him. He woke up to me tearing him apart with every curse word I could think of. And yet, he had the audacity to sit there and deny the evidence, trying to claim innocence despite the photos staring back at him. I grabbed his clothes and threw them out, screaming at him to get out of my house.

The next two to three weeks were a blur of pain, arguments, and the slow breakdown of our marriage. He clung to me, desperately trying to hold on while still maintaining his affair, trying to create a twisted scenario where we were supposed to fight for him like he was some prize. It was delusional. Then, in one moment, it felt like a switch had been flipped. I felt nothing—no love, no hate—just a stillness as I watched him spiral, grasping at anything material or monetary to try to pull me back into the chaos of his world. I stood firm in my power, rejecting every attempt he made. I let go of everything and told him to take it all, because the only thing I wanted was my children, my peace of mind, and to get as far away from him as possible.

For two months, he did everything he could think of to win me back. He even got my name tattooed on his neck and the words "married to Sara" on his ring finger, even though he never wore a wedding ring while we were together, claiming it gave him a rash. On New Year's Eve, he broke into my house, convinced that I was sleeping with someone else and trying to shift the blame for the breakdown of our marriage onto me, accusing me of infidelity when I wasn't even doing anything. I was just sleeping. He lingered around my house like an unwanted presence, constantly pestering me to let him in, claiming he just wanted to "talk," knocking on my window at all hours of the night. I ignored him and called the police, but they never responded unless it was an emergency.

Then, he used my daughter to get in. He knocked on her window, and without understanding the full situation, she let him in. I heard the noise and rushed to check, only to find him halfway through the window. I grabbed my phone to call the police again, but before I could, he chased after me, picked me up, and threw me to the ground, taking my phone and slipping it into his pocket. His demeanor shifted, his gaze softened, and his voice became quieter as he subtly begged me to talk to him.

I quickly began to assess the situation, trying to figure out how to handle things in a way that would give me the best outcome. By this point, my boys had woken up and were jumping on the bed, distracting my ex-husband. I noticed this opportunity and used it to my advantage, stealthily taking my phone back from his pocket without him realizing. I tried to call the police again, keeping the phone hidden under the blanket, hoping the dispatcher would listen in and send help. But they hung up on me twice. At that point, I decided the best way to get what I needed was to play along with him. I said, "You really upset our daughter, let me put her back to sleep and you put the boys to bed, then we can talk." He agreed.

I took my daughter back to her room and calmly told her I was going to call the police, but asked her to talk to them for me. She was happy to help, unaware of the gravity of the situation, and I made sure not to make it seem too serious. I asked her to tell the police that Daddy had come through the window and hit me and that we needed help. I knew the police would likely respond faster if a child was involved, and I didn't want her to exaggerate, just stick to the basics. I left her to it and returned to the room, where he was still putting the boys to bed, but he came back within seconds. It turned out he wasn't interested in talking, he was hoping for one last chance to sleep with me.

I needed to stall until the police arrived, so I started with the rug burn as a distraction. I put on an act, pretending to be hurt, saying, "You hurt me, now I have these burns and I need to put cream on them." I did it slowly, chuckling to myself internally as I saw how eager he was. He looked like a starving puppy waiting for a treat. After applying the cream, I claimed I needed to wash my hands, which I did slowly, almost like I was performing surgery. More giggles in my head. Then I said I needed to use the toilet and sat in there for a while, knowing he'd start to get impatient. Sure enough, he knocked on the door, asking if I was done. I yelled back, but I made sure not to overdo it, so he wouldn't get angry.

Finally, I finished up, flushed, and came out, saying, "Wait, I need to wash my hands again." The giggles continued as I dragged it out. And then, finally, I heard it—"POLICE!" They knocked on the door. I bolted past him and opened it, and the look of defeat on his face was absolutely priceless.

My ex-husband finally started to realize that I wasn't falling for his childish games anymore, and the night he gave up was when he found out I had moved on. I was enjoying a peaceful evening with someone new. The night felt young, but there was this strange, unsettling energy in the air, we both sensed it. It was as if something was about to happen, and it felt unavoidable. As we were saying goodnight and stepping outside to hug before he left, we noticed someone lurking behind my recycling bin. It was my ex-husband. He suddenly jumped out, ready to confront and fight the man I was with, completely unaware that the man I was with was highly trained in Muay Thai and could have easily handled him, but chose not to.

What followed was a brief scuffle that ended with both of them on the ground. The man I was with managed to subdue my ex-husband without causing harm, using his strength to calm him down and assert control. My ex-husband, realizing he was outmatched, backed off and started walking away, crying and shouting abusive words at me. I stood there in stunned silence, unable to react in time as it all happened so quickly.

Once my ex-husband left, the man I was with stayed for a while, just to make sure I was safe and that my ex wouldn't return. We waited for the police to arrive, ensuring my safety before he finally left.

"To embrace the new dawn is to welcome hope wrapped in light—a chance to shed old shadows and step boldly into the promise of becoming."

# CHAPTER 5:
# EMBRACING THE NEW DAWN

The sun was rising on a new chapter of my life, and I had no idea what it would bring, but I knew I was finally free to write my own story. It was funny, I'd been a married single mother for years. But now, with the weight of that title lifted, I could finally breathe. I was no longer tethered to the past, and for the first time in over a decade, I felt the spark of possibility flicker in my chest. At 27, after 11 years of being with the same man, who I had met when I was just 16, I was stepping into the unknown, as both a single mother and a woman rediscovering herself. My entire adult life had been defined by someone else's choices, but now, as I faced the daunting yet exhilarating world of singlehood, I felt the first true sense of freedom I'd ever known. It wasn't easy, and it wasn't quick, but I knew that every day I was walking away from the shadows of my past, toward a future where I was in control of my own happiness. The dawn was finally here, and I was ready to rise.

In June of 2016, I received the long-awaited paperwork in the mail that confirmed our divorce was final. I was flooded with a sense of relief and joy, knowing I would never have to deal with him again. Now, I know what you're thinking, what about the kids? Doesn't he want to be in their lives? Well, no. He told me, and I quote, "You can have them. They'll find me when they're older." Honestly, I was at peace with that. I realized it was far better for my children to have no father than one who was a constant disappointment and absent in every meaningful way. I didn't want his chaotic influence in their lives.

I knew I was strong enough to handle motherhood on my own, especially since I had already been doing it for the past eight years. And more than that, I was determined to give my kids the kind of childhood I had always wished for, one full of love, attention, nurturing, and care. So, when I finally broke free from this man, I threw a divorce party to celebrate not just getting rid of the emotional parasite who had drained me for so long, but also to honor my own strength and determination to start fresh. I called up my girlfriends, hit the town, and partied like it was 1999.

2016 was a transformative year for me, a year of reclaiming my freedom from the mental prison I had been trapped in for so long, built from years of childhood conditioning. For most of my life, I felt like I wasn't living for myself, I was living for everyone else: my parents, my sisters, my husband, my friends, and even acquaintances. But deep down, I knew I was meant to live for myself and my children. It was time for me to step into my own life, to experience the things I had longed for.

I finally felt like I was ready to embrace the world like the playground God created for his children was waiting for me to explore. 2016 became my year of firsts. I took my first road trip, went on my first bushwalk, saw my first waterfall, got my first tattoo, did my first professional photo shoot, and traveled to Melbourne for the first time from Auckland. It was an incredible year, and I cherished every single moment of it. I went on dates and realized that I had options, something my ex-husband had always made me doubt. He once made me believe I would never find anyone who would love me the way he did. But in my mind, that was exactly the point: I didn't want *his* kind of love. I wanted real love, the kind of love I had always freely given to others, the kind I deserved for myself. So I made it my mission to figure out what that looked like and to fight for it.

Over the next few years, I made it my top priority to take care of myself because I understood that my inner state directly impacts my external world. Since my children are part of that world, I knew I had to ensure I wasn't projecting any anger, discomfort, or unnecessary drama onto them. My happiness, peace, and comfort became my focus. I realized that many women today believe self-sacrifice is the key to love, but I felt differently, and I couldn't quite understand why this belief was so widespread. I always thought, "What about me? I deserve to be loved, appreciated, and cared for, just like anyone else." This sparked my curiosity, so I dove into understanding why so many women associate self-sacrifice with love. I've always been someone who questions everything; I couldn't accept something unless I understood it or it made sense to me. Despite the societal conditioning that tried to tell me otherwise, I always saw myself as a queen. I was constantly searching for what was best for me, knowing that whatever benefited me would ultimately benefit my children as well. I became a woman on a mission, not just to free myself, but to help other women break free from the patriarchal systems that society has built to keep women trapped in an energy of servitude.

Even though I had gained a sense of freedom from my ex-husband and was now free to pursue my own goals, there was still something holding me back from feeling fully liberated. I made it my mission to identify what that was and make the changes necessary to achieve complete freedom. I realized that the key to my freedom lay in understanding myself, my story, my personal journey, and the deeper mechanisms that shaped who I was as a human being. Whenever I had a moment to myself, I dedicated it to research, seeking answers, and striving for a deeper understanding. I couldn't accept the idea that my life would amount to nothing more than being a mother, a wife, a daughter, and a sister. I knew I had far more potential, and I believed I could be just as great as anyone in history who made their mark. I was determined to figure out how to achieve that greatness. The process was incredibly challenging, emotionally, mentally, and physically draining, but my perseverance never wavered. I felt an unmatched drive within me; I was always someone who took action, while everyone around me just talked about their dreams without taking any steps to make them real.

Gradually, I began to notice more. I started paying closer attention to what was really happening around me. At the time, I didn't fully understand it, but now I see that I was constantly being kept in a state of distraction through doing. There was always something or someone demanding my attention, whether it was my job as a nurse, my patients, my kids, my parents, my sisters, university work, or house responsibilities. You name it, I was handling it. And as someone who's always been a go-getter, it all felt normal, almost second nature.

But even in the midst of all that "normal," I could feel something was missing. No matter how much I accomplished, everything felt surface-level, driven by external expectations rather than true fulfillment. I knew I had to dig deeper into myself. I started to feel the urgency like my life depended on it. Eventually, I hit a breaking point. I was stretched impossibly thin; working two jobs, running a side hustle, completing a master's degree, managing a household, and raising three children on my own, each with their own unique needs and personalities. On top of that, I was caring for my elderly parents and stepping in whenever my sisters needed something. My ex-husband was completely absent, both physically and financially.

And yet, I did it all with a smile on my face and a pep in my step, that was the mask I wore. I kept up the illusion that everything was fine, that I had it all under control. But the truth was, I was burying my own emotions just to make space for everyone else's and it was quietly tearing me apart.

It was July 2023, just three months away from finishing my Master's degree, when everything hit a breaking point. The pressure had become unbearable, the academic demands were outrageous, and the payoff in my field was barely worth the stress. That realization hit me hard during what felt like a quiet, internal mental breakdown. The thought of pushing through made me physically sick. So, in my mind, I screamed, *"I QUIT."*

And I meant it. I made an executive decision to walk away from it all. I withdrew from my degree, shut down my business, and quit one of my two jobs. A few months later, I left the second one as well. I sold almost everything I owned and moved into my parents' house with my three kids. At the time, my mother was already in Melbourne helping my sister, and my dad had gone to visit too. The original plan was for me to move to Melbourne as well but that was stalled by my father's irrational fears and his need to control the situation.

So, I stayed back. I lived rent-free in my parents' house for seven months, hitting pause on everything before finally making the move I'd been planning.

My father constantly offloaded his irrational fears onto me, and without question, I absorbed the weight of them. I had been so deeply conditioned to abandon my own needs and feelings in order to cater to him that I responded almost robotically. When he insisted I stay back to "watch the house," I complied. Despite the fact that it had an alarm system, watchful neighbors, a low fence facing a busy reserve, and full insurance coverage. None of that mattered to him. In his mind, it still wasn't safe unless *I* was there to protect it.

While my family gathered in Melbourne, celebrating milestones like my nephew's first birthday, I was left behind, once again, excluded from meaningful family moments. I've often felt like an outsider in my own family. The black sheep. The burden they tolerated because we were "family," but rarely ever made to feel like I belonged. That version of family, lacking in love, care, and genuine consideration, was far from what I believed family should be. Being asked to stay behind for the sake of a house, while everyone else enjoyed being together, hurt deeply.

Still, I chose to look for the silver lining. I decided to take that time as a chance to pause and reflect, to really sit with my emotions and explore what was going on beneath the surface. Those seven months became pivotal in my transformation. I had saved enough money to carry me through that period, rent-free, only needing to cover food and bills, which allowed me to do something I had never done before: nothing. I finally had space to *just be.*

You'd think, given my circumstances, that my father would recognize the load I was carrying and offer to lighten it. But instead, he added to it. The imbalance between how he treated me versus my sisters was glaring. He liked to make it seem like he was supporting me, reminding me of the time he paid off a $3K loan, the car he bought me for graduation, or the temporary financial help of $200–300 a week for a short while. But that paled in comparison to what my sisters received, multiple cars, and $10,000 to $20,000 each when they moved to Melbourne to help them transition.

The difference wasn't just in the money, it was in the energy, the intention, the care. And I felt it. It felt like he was punishing me for resisting the control he had so effortlessly exerted over my sisters. At the time, I didn't yet understand narcissism, so I dismissed his behavior as simple paranoia or fearfulness. In many ways, I've always seen my father as a pathetic, overgrown toddler, someone who threw tantrums whenever things didn't go his way. Sometimes, it seemed like he threw tantrums just for the sake of it. One vivid example was when I walked into my parents' home during a heated argument between them. He was furiously accusing my mother of using his debit card, even though he had supposedly told her to only use the credit card. As I entered, they both turned to me and asked if I knew anything about it. I calmly said, "Yes, Dad used it when we went to buy honey. The store didn't accept credit cards." He paused, realizing he had just berated my mother over something he himself had done. But instead of owning up to it and apologizing, he did what narcissists often do, he spun it into a lecture. He barked at my mother to take this outburst as a lesson: never use his debit card again, lest he throw another fit.

I had always harbored a deep hatred for my father. To me, he was cruel, dismissive, and utterly unbearable to be around. Our entire household revolved around catering to his every whim, home of four women who were barely allowed to exist for fear that one of us might steal the spotlight from the overgrown child we were forced to tiptoe around. By the time I became a teenager, the atmosphere felt suffocating. I was like a caged animal, desperate to escape the grasp of this man who made me feel like my only purpose was to serve him. I couldn't take it anymore. So, with the help of my then-boyfriend, and later my first husband, I made a plan to leave. One night at 17, I packed my things, climbed out of my bedroom window, and ran away. Before leaving, I wrote my father a long letter filled with the hatred I had bottled up for years, making sure he would know just how much I despised him. But my mother and sister found it first and threw it away, so he never read it.

For a brief moment, I felt free, like I could finally live life on my own terms. But I was wrong. I had simply escaped one kind of hell only to step into another. My boyfriend turned out to be yet another narcissist, unsurprisingly. Still, I couldn't go back. Returning would have meant giving my father the satisfaction of seeing me crawl back after the way I had left. So I stayed, choosing the lesser of two evils. At least with my boyfriend, I had some, however small, control over my own life, something I never had under my father's rule.

I endured years of torment, not just from my family, but later from my husband and his family as well. I was left bewildered, unable to understand why the people who were supposed to love me treated me like I was nothing. I approached them with innocence, perhaps even naivety but how could I not, growing up in such a warped environment? All I ever wanted was to love them and be loved in return. Was that really too much to ask? Was I so inherently unlovable that everyone meant to care for me chose instead to hurt me?

I bent over backward to meet everyone else's needs. I never completely abandoned my own, but I constantly put theirs ahead of mine whenever conflict arose. All I ever longed for was to be loved gently, to be spoken to with kindness, to be nurtured, to feel like I mattered. These thoughts consumed me when I finally broke free from my husband and began to stand on my own. That moment marked the beginning of my awakening, the painful realization of the kind of family I came from and the pattern of abuse I had unknowingly accepted for far too long.

"In the house of silence and shadows, truths whisper softly—waiting to be heard, understood, and finally set free."

# CHAPTER 6:
# THE HOUSE OF SILENCE
# AND SHADOWS

After I left my husband, I went back to my parents' home thinking it would be a place of safety, maybe even healing. But the moment I walked through that front door, the air felt the same, thick with tension, heavy with things never said. I sat at the kitchen table, listening to my father bark orders like he was the king of a crumbling castle, while my mother moved around like a ghost trying not to be seen. It hit me slowly, then all at once: this wasn't refuge, this was where the damage began. I didn't escape abuse. I returned to its birthplace. I thought I had escaped the worst when I left my husband, but returning to my parents' home was like stepping back into the original wound. The abuse didn't start with him, it started in the silence of that house, in the way love was withheld, in the way my voice never mattered. I didn't recognize it at first, because it was disguised as normal. It was home.

I want to be clear, I didn't move back in with my parents. I still had my own place. But I returned to my family seeking comfort, hoping for support and solace. I was under the illusion that I could lean on them emotionally, though, in hindsight, I don't know why I ever believed that. Looking back, I realize I never actually received emotional support from them. In our family, we were always walking on eggshells around each other's feelings. I learned early on that mine didn't matter. Instead, I was expected to make space for my father's and my oldest sister's emotions while ignoring my own.

They were the most reactive people in the family, you couldn't say anything without triggering an outburst. My father would yell, and my sister would dissolve into tears. It was always their way or no way at all. God help us if they receive even the slightest criticism.

I remember one night at dinner, we were discussing politics. I expressed my support for the Labor Party, largely because of their focus on helping the poor access basic resources and support. I believe that reducing inequality would also reduce crime, as people wouldn't need to resort to desperate measures to survive. My sister, on the other hand, supported the National Party. She felt she had worked hard her whole life and deserved to keep the majority of her earnings rather than fund social programs. While I could understand her perspective to an extent, I challenged it as selfish. I argued that society has a responsibility to support the vulnerable, including those struggling with mental illness, not only out of compassion but for the stability and safety of all.

The conversation escalated quickly, not because of our disagreement, but because she couldn't handle being challenged. My father eventually yelled at her to drop it and said I was right. To me, it was just a conversation, a difference of opinion. I wasn't trying to win, nor did I take it personally. But she had an emotional meltdown, crying that our father didn't take her side. I didn't understand her reaction at the time, I've never been one to take things that seriously. But now I see she was constantly seeking our father's approval, something I never cared much about. In retrospect, it makes sense why she never liked me.

My family home never felt like a true home to me, it felt more like a cage, a circus of sorts. Each child was like an animal locked in their own room, with my father as the ringmaster, controlling everything, and my mother as his ever-obedient assistant. I always felt different from the rest of my family, separate, like the odd one out, the black sheep who refused to conform. I didn't fall into the same cycles that seemed to trap my sisters and mother in their dance with my father's rules. I was always the one to speak out, to reject their ideals, to openly disagree. I rebelled against everything they tried to instill in me, everything they believed was the "right" way to live. It made no sense to me; it all seemed pointless.

Growing up, I often felt like an outsider, watching everyone live their lives in this uncomfortable, secretive way where no one truly knew anyone else. We all had to pretend to like each other, to get along, but the tension was palpable. It was no surprise that everyone retreated to their rooms, avoiding the chaos. The atmosphere was suffocating, dominated by my father's anger, always simmering beneath the surface, a ticking time bomb ready to explode. My mother, on the other hand, was like a ghost, quietly floating around, trying to keep the peace and hold the family together, maintaining the illusion of a perfect home. She seemed to take such pride in being married to a doctor, eager to project this image of the perfect, middle-class family.

My two older sisters were driven, overachievers with egos as large as the sky. My oldest sister would never shop at a regular store. No, she needed only the most expensive, high-quality items, feeding her obsession with shoes. She had three closets full of heels! To her, looking wealthy and successful was everything; it was the only way she could feel loved and accepted, especially by our father. Her desperate need for his approval was both painfully obvious and heartbreaking. I couldn't help but feel sorry for her.

Then there was my middle sister, her rage was buried deep beneath the surface. Nothing was ever good enough for our father. She'd work tirelessly for straight A's, but if she brought home a B in a sea of A's, it was like a betrayal. How dare she get a B? It was never enough. I could never understand why my sisters were so hungry to please him while I saw him as a monster I couldn't wait to escape. I brought home C's, and I couldn't care less about his approval. I didn't study. When they locked me in my room with an open textbook, I would take a nap instead. They'd come back to find the book untouched, still on the same page they left it. No amount of yelling, shaming, or judgment could move me. I just didn't care. And they would always say, "You're so smart but so lazy!"

What they didn't realize was that I already knew how smart I was, not in an arrogant way, but in a way that was grounded in self-trust. I've always just followed what felt right for me. I hated the life I was living with them because it was all so fake. The love was fake, the respect was fake, the sense of togetherness was fake, and everything about it felt hollow. I was the only real thing in the fake world they had created, and that I had been born into. I could never understand why I had to pretend to be something I wasn't. I didn't want to play this game of who's the best at pretending, who could fake it the most convincingly. I wanted to be real, to be myself, and to be accepted for who I truly was, not for the version they wanted me to be. But I suppose asking for that was too much.

They kept pushing, trying to shrink me, trying to force me to conform, to follow their misguided path. I was like a wild animal they wanted to tame, to leash, but they didn't realize that as the third child, I knew they were too tired, too worn out to try any harder than they already had. It was like a psychological tug-of-war for control. They thought they won each small battle, but I was playing a much bigger game, I was in it to win the war.

Returning to that house as an adult, a woman who had been married, had three children, and gone through a divorce, felt completely surreal. It was like stepping back onto a psychological battlefield, and this time, I was determined to win. Inside me, two conflicting forces were constantly at war. On one side, I craved absolute freedom, from everyone, even family, if the connection lacked honesty, openness, and depth. I just wanted to escape. But I felt trapped, conditioned from a young age to abandon myself in order to meet the needs of others.

On the other side, whenever I was physically away from these people, I channeled all my energy into self-care, research, and personal growth. I was fiercely committed to understanding myself and breaking free from the mental chains that had kept me stuck for so long. Still, something in me kept getting pulled back to my parents' house, a place of shadows and silence, where I always felt like I was circling the same emotional loop. Deep down, I knew that until I could fully liberate myself from that cycle, I'd never feel truly free.

It wasn't all bad, we had our moments. There were times of joy and laughter, though more often than not, I was the one who initiated them. I brought light into the darkness of their unspoken pain. In many ways, I felt like an overworked, unpaid, and unappreciated therapist to my parents. I often felt more like a parent than they ever were to me. I could see the pain and loneliness etched into my father's face, and sometimes, just to lift his spirits, I'd ask him a question, usually something related to health or medicine, because I knew how much he loved to talk about it. I'd ask something simple, often connected to my own work as a nurse prescriber, and he'd launch into a long-winded explanation. I didn't ask because I needed the information, I asked because I wanted him to feel like his thoughts mattered like his opinion had value.

I knew I couldn't change him or heal him, but I still wanted to offer him a little light. I sacrificed a lot of my time and energy for my dad, not just because I felt obligated, though that was part of it, but also because a part of me genuinely wanted to. I've always carried a strong motherly energy, seeing the child in everyone, no matter their age. Their behaviors, often immature or emotionally underdeveloped, would trigger something in me, a subconscious instinct to nurture, to guide, to hold space. I found myself slipping into the role of caretaker for anyone who seemed lost in the darkness of their own mind.

I had a gift for lightening the mood, for bringing a flicker of joy to people just by engaging them in what they loved to talk about. But I hated feeling responsible for that role in my family. It was far too heavy a burden for one person to carry, and the truth is, it never should have been mine to bear in the first place.

For a long time, I felt an obligation to visit my father every week, believing it was necessary for his mental well-being. I wanted to be there for him, someone he could talk to, engage with, and go out with, so he wouldn't be consumed by the isolation of his own home. But the truth is, I hated being around him. His presence was draining, filled with negative energy. He was overbearing, always demanding to be the center of attention. No one else could speak when he did, and everything he said was right, no matter the evidence to the contrary. I found myself sacrificing my peace, my time, and my emotional energy to meet his needs, while enduring the discomfort of his toxic atmosphere. I resented feeling like I had no choice, and I was desperate to understand why I felt this way and how to break free from it because I was utterly miserable.

For years, I operated on autopilot, weighed down by an invisible force that kept me constantly on standby, always waiting for the next request from a family member. I became the go-to person, the reliable one. From a young age, I was running errands for my sisters in exchange for small rewards like candy. That soon escalated to supermarket runs for my mother and sisters, tracking down information they needed, finding tradesmen, comparing prices, posting parcels, chauffeuring my parents to appointments, doing their shopping, or simply taking them out for leisure, often to the beach.

The cycle of doing never stopped. It was second nature to me; I was wired to get things done. I wasn't one to sit around talking about plans, I lived by the motto: "Make like Nike and Just do it." There was no time to pause, reflect, or consider alternatives. Responsibility had been placed on my shoulders from such a young age that becoming a parent at 19 almost felt like a natural extension of the role I'd always played. I had been mothering my entire family through acts of service, and in return, I was given money or material things, a form of transactional love.

Without realizing it, I had become their personal assistant, efficiently managing their lives while trying to juggle my own and care for my children. I don't know how I managed to keep it all together, presenting a façade of ease while silently enduring the emotional toll. Every now and then, I would collapse, mentally and emotionally, alone in my room, out of sight. That's what was expected of me. I wasn't allowed to take up space or tend to my own emotional needs. I was conditioned to be invisible, to hold space only for the feelings of others.

My breaking point came in July 2023, I simply couldn't do it anymore. I was juggling two jobs, running a side hustle, pushing through a demanding master's degree, caring for my three children, managing my household, visiting my father weekly to tend to his needs, and occasionally supporting my mother while she was in Melbourne helping my sister. By then, most of my "personal assistant" energy was directed toward my father.

But that was it. I'd reached my limit. I quit one of the jobs, withdrew from my degree, shut down my business, sold most of my belongings, and started preparing to finally move to Melbourne. I wasn't just looking for a change of scenery, I needed to reclaim my life. I was determined to soften the pace, focus on myself, and break free from the mental prison that kept me trapped in this cycle of serving others while sidelining my own needs and dreams. I wanted to live *for myself*. It was my life, and I deserved to live it on my own terms, not according to what my family expected of me.

By September 2023, I was ready to go. That was the plan. But of course, my father had other ideas. He insisted I delay the move so he could travel to Melbourne himself, to enjoy the spring, and summer, and celebrate my nephew's first birthday. And just like that, I was expected to stay behind, to "look after" his house while he was away. He was paranoid about being robbed, despite having a house alarm, watchful neighbors, a home in a busy area, and full insurance coverage.

Once again, I was obligated to put my life on hold because I'd been conditioned to believe I had no choice. It was absurd. And yet, I stayed because that's the role I had always played. I felt isolated, yet again excluded from the rest of the family. It's no wonder I never truly felt like I belonged, I was always the one left behind.

I wasn't the type to complain, I always tried to stay focused on the bright side, to find the silver lining. So I buried how I really felt, knowing deep down I wouldn't be heard anyway. Instead, I used those seven extra months I was forced to stay behind as an opportunity to work on myself. I continued working until December 2023, all while living at my parents' house, a surreal experience, considering I hadn't lived there since I was 17. You'd think my father might show some compassion, knowing I was a single mother of three, trying to provide for my family and plan a major move. Instead, he demanded I pay over a thousand dollars toward his annual property taxes, justifying it by saying I was staying there "rent-free" as if that somehow made sense when it was his idea for me to stay. On top of that, he charged me for all the bills: electricity, water, internet—you name it.

The living situation itself was far from comfortable. He had his computer and a pile of clutter dominating the family room, making the space feel chaotic and closed in. I wasn't allowed to move anything and was expected to just sit in the discomfort, literally and emotionally. Eventually, I rearranged things anyway and braced myself for the backlash when he returned. At that point, I didn't care. He clearly had no concern for my comfort, so why should I prioritize his?

Every day, I dove deep into self-exploration, reading, researching, and reflecting. It felt like one revelation after another, each one peeling back layers of who I thought I was and who I had been conditioned to be. It was painful, emotional, and at times overwhelming, but it was also deeply empowering. I was finally getting to know myself, finally breaking free from the mental prison I had been living in for so long.

During this time, I leaned on my herbal medicine, marijuana, which I used daily. It gave me the clarity I needed to quiet the noise of all the programming I'd been subjected to growing up. For the first time, I was thinking for myself. And that sense of liberation? It was everything.

The house that had once been filled with silence and shadows was, for those seven months, alive with light, love, and energy. During that time, I began to see clearly that the life I had been living wasn't truly mine, it never had been. I was finally in the process of reclaiming it. I had to unlearn so much, to rediscover who I was beneath all the layers of conditioning, expectations, and self-limiting beliefs. It was a rebirth, a transformation. Each day, I peeled back another layer of mental noise, dismantling the thoughts and patterns that had kept me trapped in a life dictated by the needs and desires of others.

I was breaking down to rebuild, deliberately, fiercely. I was unstoppable in my commitment to change. This was *my* life, and whatever was going to be mine had to be self-created. The inner work wasn't optional, it was necessary. It was now or never, because I knew I wouldn't be here forever.

I had spent far too many years neglecting myself, pouring my energy outward without pause. But the realization hit hard: attention is the true currency of our existence. Wherever I chose to place it was shaping my reality. I was no longer willing to invest it in everyone but myself. That was the moment I became loud, bright, and unapologetically alive.

"Breaking the cycle is the courageous journey of peeling away the past—finding strength in every fracture, and reclaiming the self beneath the pain."

# CHAPTER 7:
# BREAKING THE CYCLE:
# A JOURNEY BACK TO ME

I remember standing in the middle of my father's living room, staring at the clutter he refused to move. It wasn't just the physical mess that made me uneasy, it was what it symbolized. That room was a reflection of what my life had become: cramped, chaotic, dictated by someone else's rules. For years, I tiptoed around other people's emotions, sacrificing my comfort to maintain their peace. But at that moment, something shifted. I quietly moved the furniture. I made space. Not just in the room, but in myself. It was a small act of rebellion, but for me, it was the first brick laid on the path back to my own life.

"Sometimes, breaking the cycle doesn't start with a scream, it starts with a quiet decision: I deserve better than this."

I was a woman on a mission, not just to rediscover who I was, but to reclaim a life that had been taken from me, piece by piece, over the years. I threw myself into the work of healing, unlearning, and rebuilding. It all began with one book that shifted everything: *The Myth of Normal* by Dr. Gabor Maté. That book cracked something open in me. It challenged everything I thought was "just the way things are." For the first time, I saw the patterns clearly, and I knew there had to be more to life than what I had been conditioned to accept as normal.

I couldn't believe I had been led to think my sole purpose was to serve—serve men, be a good wife, a dutiful daughter, a reliable sister, and a compliant member of society. A people-pleaser who constantly abandoned herself in the hope that someone might one day notice her worth and offer back the same love, care, and effort she so freely gave. That narrative wasn't just limited, it was dehumanizing. And I refused to keep living inside that lie. It wasn't my truth, and it was never going to be my life.

If you've ever questioned why so many people struggle with anxiety, illness, or burnout in a society that calls itself "advanced," this book will resonate deeply. In *The Myth of Normal*, Dr. Gabor Maté dismantles the idea that our modern culture promotes wellness. Instead, he shows how trauma, disconnection, and stress are baked into what we call "normal life", and how that "normal" is making us sick.

You'll love this book if you're drawn to thoughtful critiques of societal norms, interested in the intersection of mental and physical health, or are on a personal journey of healing. Maté writes with deep compassion and clarity, blending scientific insight with human stories. It's part revelation, part roadmap for reclaiming authenticity and connection in a world that often suppresses both.

My parents' religion, Islam, as it was practiced and enforced in my household, felt less like a path to divine connection and more like a system of control, especially over women. It functioned as a framework designed by men, for men, to extract from the feminine, emotionally, spiritually, and energetically. It wasn't about love or healing; it was about fear, obedience, and keeping me dependent. The more afraid and depleted I was, the easier it was to keep me small, silent, and in service.

They didn't want me empowered or whole, they wanted me loyal, drained, and desperate for love that was always dangled just out of reach. It was a false light: warm and comforting as long as I conformed, but cold and punishing the moment I questioned or tried to leave. My role was never to thrive, it was to give, to serve, to sustain everyone else. That's how I became the unpaid personal assistant of the family, a role I never chose.

Looking back, it felt like an energetic ambush. My pain and vulnerability were observed, studied, and then used, not to support me, but to extract what little light I had left. Whether they knew it or not, this was a form of spiritual and emotional vampirism disguised as duty and community. I understand this might sound strange to those who haven't explored their spiritual side, but for me, and for many others walking this path of awakening, it makes perfect sense.

Whether my family was consciously aware of what they were doing, or simply acting as unconscious participants in a larger pattern, what some might call "NPCs," non-player characters following inherited programming, the result is the same. The harm was real. And I've come to accept that I can't heal in environments that are committed to misunderstanding me.

The seven months I spent back at my parents' house became a pivotal chapter in my transformation. Though it was never part of the plan, that time brought me closer to myself in ways I couldn't have imagined. It felt paradoxical, time passed quickly, yet every day moved slowly like I was wading through emotional molasses. But in that stillness, something sacred began to unfold.

Each day, I'd smoke a blunt and sit with my thoughts, not to escape them, but to truly listen. I challenged what came up, questioned everything I believed, and researched endlessly to understand where those beliefs came from. I held a deep knowing: *the only way to truly let something go is to understand it first.* I started to see healing like assembling flat-pack furniture. If you try to build something without instructions, you'll likely make mistakes, feel frustrated, and start over multiple times. But with guidance, even if it's improvised, you eventually figure it out.

I didn't have a manual for healing, but I had my own willingness to take it step by step. I approached myself gently, patiently, and with compassion, qualities I had always reserved for others but rarely extended to myself. This time, I flipped the script. I gave myself what I had spent a lifetime giving away: attention, love, and care. And yes, I knew it would disappoint the people who had grown used to feeding off that energy, but I no longer cared. It was my turn.

It wasn't selfish to want for myself what I so freely offered others. It was necessary. Life doesn't wait, and I didn't want to spend the rest of mine starving for peace, waiting for someone else to give me what I had the power to give myself. So I did. I chose me. And I accepted, fully and finally, that those meant to walk with me would, and those who weren't would fall away. So be it.

If I was going to matter, if I was going to truly *exist*, then I had to include myself in the living. I was done being a robot, a ghost, a people-pleasing version of myself waiting on the next command. I'm here now. Fully.

Through months of consistent research, reading books, watching YouTube videos, scrolling through TikToks, and absorbing wisdom from experts in the self-help and healing space, I began to find the answers I had been searching for. I needed things to *make sense* before I could truly let them go. My top priority was freeing myself from the emotional grip my parents, particularly my father, had on me. Their influence weighed heaviest on my spirit, and I instinctively knew that understanding them was the first key to loosening that hold.

That's what led me down the path of studying narcissism and people-pleasing. I knew that to escape the mental prison I'd been trapped in, I had to understand the environment I was raised in, and the soil I was planted in. And that soil? It was toxic. I couldn't grow into the woman I was becoming without first replacing that soil with something nourishing, safe, and self-honoring. I needed to replant myself in healthier ground, sowing new seeds of thought that would one day bloom into peace, power, and purpose.

I can't even count how many articles, books, and videos I consumed on narcissism, especially to understand my father. It was eye-opening. Every behavior I read about, every pattern described, was like a mirror reflecting back my childhood and young adulthood. I finally saw it clearly: he was a physically grown man, but emotionally stunted like a toddler in an adult's body, playing the role of a parent.

One moment that perfectly captured this was a day we were grocery shopping together. He bought a Kit Kat and, as I was loading the bags into the car, he turned to me and asked, "Where should I put my chocolate?" I remember blinking at him, baffled. He was a grown man, a doctor, no less and he was asking his daughter where to put a candy bar. I shrugged and said, "Just put it in your pocket." He immediately protested, saying it would melt. I said nothing further, assuming he'd figure it out.

But a few minutes later, he asked again. At that point, I was confused. This was such a simple problem, yet he seemed completely incapable of solving it on his own. I repeated my response and added that if it melted, he could just put it in the fridge later or simply hold it in his hand. That's when he snapped, threw the chocolate into the boot of the car in a small tantrum, and stormed off to the passenger seat, sulking.

I couldn't help but laugh, not out of cruelty, but because the moment was so absurd. This was the man who had tried to dominate every conversation, and control every decision, and yet couldn't figure out what to do with a Kit Kat. That was the moment it really hit me: I had spent my whole life seeking approval from someone who was emotionally unequipped to even care for himself properly, let alone guide me.

It was, to say the least, deeply embarrassing, not for me, but for him. There were countless moments where I genuinely felt more like the parent, and he the child. Eventually, I began to piece things together and realized that people who operate primarily from their ego are often just overgrown children, adults in appearance, but emotionally stunted with a childlike mindset. This became especially clear during one particular exchange. I asked him, "If you have a problem and want it resolved, why not just express it calmly? We could talk it through and find a solution together, instead of you yelling and throwing tantrums every time you're upset."

Rather than responding constructively, he shouted back at me, furious that I would dare to tell him how to behave. "Who do you think you are, trying to raise me now? I'm already grown. I'll do whatever I please, whether you like it or not," he snapped. I took a breath and replied simply, "Okay. Well, every time you start yelling at me, I'll just leave. You can yell at the wall instead." And that's exactly what I did. He continued trying to dominate conversations with raised voices, but I began walking out and going home. After a few times, he started to realize that his yelling only pushed me further away.

In response, he began scrambling to find new ways to assert control and feed his ego. Over time, I started pulling back, not just from him, but from my family as a whole. Where I once visited multiple times a week, I cut it down to once, and eventually even that visit shrank from an entire day to just a couple of hours. This gradual distancing continued until February 2024, when both he and my mother returned from Melbourne to Auckland. By then, my seven-month stay at their house was ending, and I was finally preparing to move to Melbourne.

This was the moment everything changed, the turning point where the power dynamics shifted, and everything my father had controlled and dominated for as long as I could remember began to crumble. He was no longer the powerful figure he had been, but instead a sad, desperate man. It was the day of their return. I had worked tirelessly to clean, stock, and prepare the house for them. Exhausted, I knew I still had to pick them up from the airport at 2 a.m., even though I had been awake since 5 a.m. I was barely functioning, a half-asleep zombie, trying to drive to the airport to cater to their need for comfort, so they wouldn't have to take an Uber or taxi and could instead be driven by family.

My fatigue was obvious, my eyes were barely open, with dark circles under them, yawning constantly. Any compassionate person would have seen that and asked if I was okay, maybe offering to take an Uber or at least expressing gratitude for the effort I was making, despite my exhaustion. But not my father. He looked at me, saw my tiredness, and immediately became upset. He questioned why I looked so drained and why I wasn't greeting them with energy and enthusiasm. He was offended by my exhaustion, turning it into an issue about him. How dare I not greet him with open arms, a smile, and a burst of joy after his arrival? In his mind, I was an ungrateful daughter, as if seven months of rent-free housing was a favor he had bestowed upon me.

Technically, I *had* paid rent in my own way, by contributing over a thousand dollars toward his property taxes. But of course, that wasn't the narrative he chose. His behavior towards me was nothing short of disgusting. He stared at me, anger etched into his face as I drove them home. Once we arrived, his tantrums started to unravel. He began yelling at me and my mother because I'd moved his clutter in the living room, then started picking apart every small change I had made. For example, I removed the bathroom curtain to let in more light. He yelled at me for not putting it back. Another thing, he noticed the two teaspoons he had stacked over his pot of honey, which he kept next to his bed for when his blood sugar dropped during the night were gone.

Months ago, I had put the spoons in the sink to be washed, thinking he wouldn't want to use spoons that had collected dust for months. It was a simple act of courtesy, a small gesture of consideration. But instead of appreciating it, he yelled, explaining that the two spoons were there specifically to protect one from the dust. I could have easily gotten two new spoons and placed them there, but that wasn't the point. He wasn't interested in solutions. He just wanted to create chaos, because deep down, he was a miserable man trying to drag us down to his nursery, because as the saying goes "misery loves company."

He continued nitpicking and yelling at everything, and eventually, I couldn't take it anymore. It was now 3 a.m., and this overgrown toddler just wouldn't stop. I had reached my breaking point. So, I snapped. I didn't have anything else to say except to scream in his face, calling him heartless.

After I exploded in response to his abusive behavior, I tuned him out and went to bed. I had no energy left to deal with his nonsense. The next morning, I woke up filled with unease, knowing I still had two more weeks in that house with him before my flight to Melbourne in early March. At that point, I was still working for a nursing agency, picking up casual shifts to make extra income for the move. I had sold my car and was relying on theirs to get to work. I made up my mind that I would simply ignore him and keep my distance to maintain peace until I could leave.

I knew he had been waiting for the day I'd return, even the slightest bit dependent on him again. He was desperate to control me, especially since I had run away from his house at 17. I could see it in his eyes, feel it in his energy, he resented the fact that he couldn't control me the way he controlled my mother and sisters. They would always defend him, even when his behavior was blatantly toxic. My sister, in particular, even claimed that his harsh way of parenting pushed her to become a high achiever, and she was *grateful* for the abuse, though she didn't recognize it for what it was.

I won't lie, though, I did feel a small sense of relief after finally standing up to him, even if it was brief. It was like I could feel my power slowly returning. Each day passed, but the tension in the house was palpable and uncomfortable. My mother kept trying to get me to take responsibility, pushing me to apologize to him and "keep the peace." She nagged at me for days, but I refused. My father, meanwhile, began grasping for control again, sending me bills to pay, through my mother, and trying to assign me tasks. I ignored him, but then he took it a step further. In front of me, he walked into his room and took the car keys, as if to say, "Figure out another way to get to work."

That was the final breaking point. I couldn't let it slide. It wasn't just an attack on me anymore, this was an attack on my ability to provide for my children. He was trying to make it harder for me to get to work, and that crossed a line. No one—*no one*—would come between a mother and her children without facing the full force of her wrath. Even in the animal kingdom, that's understood.

I immediately confronted him, "So now you're taking the keys? How petty can you be? Do you have *any* emotional intelligence, or are you just a manchild?" His response was as predictable as ever—yelling, trying to rally my mother against me. The urge to run to the bathroom was overwhelming. But it wasn't just a physical need; it felt like I was releasing 36 years of pent-up emotions that I'd never been allowed to express. As I sat there, it felt almost like an energy release, and I strangely felt powerful.

When I returned to the room, I went right back at him. Every word I had ever wanted to say just came pouring out, like verbal diarrhea. He kept trying to drag my mother and even my teenage son into his corner, but I wouldn't let him. This was between him and me, and I was holding him accountable, no matter how much he resisted. He looked at me like I was the crazy one like I was the problem, but in reality, he was completely apathetic, there wasn't a shred of concern for anyone but himself. I wasn't the crazy one for finally reacting to decades of emotional abuse. He was, and I was going to prove it to the rest of my family by letting them see it in their own time and by my refusal to shrink to appease his needs and my mother's need for peace.

"Shattering the illusions is the first breath of truth—breaking free from what deceived us to discover who we truly are."

# CHAPTER 8:
# SHATTERING THE ILLUSIONS

The outburst came like a sudden storm, a response to years of silent suffering and unspoken anger. For so long, I had lived in a fog of confusion, second-guessing my reality, excusing his cruelty, convincing myself that I was the problem. But in that heated exchange, something clicked, something snapped inside me. I had expected guilt, fear, or shame to rise up afterward, as it always did. Instead, there was a strange emptiness. The illusion that I had to earn his love or seek his approval evaporated in a single, explosive moment.

I realized that the years of emotional manipulation, the constant gaslighting, and the unrelenting demands to be something I was not, had built a house of mirrors around me. The reflection I had seen in those mirrors wasn't mine; it was a distortion of his needs, his expectations, his control. That outburst? It wasn't just a loss of temper, it was my soul finally screaming for its own space, its own truth.

In the aftermath, I didn't feel relief as I had hoped, nor did I feel victorious. What I felt was raw. But beneath that rawness, there was also something else, a flicker of self-awareness that had long been absent. For the first time in years, I began to see the person I truly was, unfiltered and untethered to the lies I had been told. The journey back to myself wasn't going to be easy, but at that moment, I had already begun.

"It wasn't just my words that shattered in that moment, it was the version of myself I had spent years trying to protect, trying to please. I thought I was defending myself, but what I didn't realize was that I was finally breaking free from the chains I had willingly worn for so long."

The days that followed that outburst were drenched in heavy tension, a thick, invisible fog of discomfort, and a quiet, ongoing power struggle. My father withdrew into silence, weaponizing it like a child sulking in the corner, all while casting himself as the victim. He took out his displaced anger on my mother, blaming her for "allowing" me to speak to him that way as if she had control over my voice or choices. It was clear he was waiting, almost obsessively, for an apology that would never come.

In his usual passive-aggressive fashion, he made subtle attempts to reassert control. He insisted we all sit and eat together as a family, suddenly placing importance on rituals he had never cared about before. He even tried to force my children to participate. I called him out, questioning why shared meals suddenly mattered to him now. That simple challenge triggered another tantrum. He exploded again, this time directing his rage at my mother, yelling that she shouldn't let me speak to him directly, further proof of his refusal to engage with me like an adult.

Despite the tension, I focused on maintaining a calm and peaceful space for myself and my children. I kept my distance, spent more time in our rooms, and took long walks with my kids to get us out of that oppressive environment. The days dragged on, but something fundamental had changed: I had reclaimed my power. I had stood up to the man who once terrified me, the man who had bullied me throughout my childhood, and I wasn't going to give him one more ounce of control.

From that moment on, I made a silent vow to myself: my needs and my children's well-being would always come first. I began to fully detach from my family of origin, emotionally and mentally. And with that detachment came something profound, peace. Freedom. The awareness that I had a choice. That my choices were mine to make. That I no longer had to carry guilt or shame for choosing myself. I was finally free.

I was finally free—free from their emotional grip, from the manipulation and control that had shaped so much of my life. But I wasn't yet free from the programming that still echoed in my mind. The noise, the constant inner chatter, the doubt, the guilt, was still there, like a familiar ghost whispering outdated messages. I realized that true peace required more than just physical distance; I needed to learn how to quiet my mind, to reclaim the space within me that had never fully been mine.

Leaving felt like shedding a massive weight I had carried for decades. For the first time in my life, I had something I'd never really known: time. Time for myself. Time to reflect, to dream, to explore the things I wanted to do, not for survival, not for anyone else, but for *me*. My attention belonged to me again, and I could finally choose where to place it. The possibilities were endless. The choices were mine.

And then it hit me—*now what?* I had spent my entire life serving others, meeting their needs, fulfilling their expectations. I had no roadmap beyond "get away." Now that I was out, I didn't know what I needed, how I felt, or who I truly was. I had always outsourced those answers to others, asking what *they* thought I should do, and what direction *they* thought I should take.

So, this became my new mission: to meet myself. To learn who I was outside the roles and rules I had been forced into. Who am I, really? Who do I want to become? And how do I create a life that's truly mine—rooted in authenticity, purpose, and peace?

"Planting new seeds is an act of faith—nurturing hope in the soil of change, trusting in growth yet to come."

# CHAPTER 9: PLANTING NEW SEEDS

For most of my life, I wore a mask I didn't know I was given, crafted from my mother's unspoken rules to serve, to please, and to disappear if it kept others comfortable. My father's narcissism taught me that love had to be earned through pain and silence. I lived trapped in their stories, thinking they were my own. But one day, the weight of pretending became heavier than the fear of facing the truth. I shattered the illusions I had mistaken for love, worth, and identity. And in the wreckage, I found the roots of who I truly was. That's when I began planting new seeds, seeds of self-worth, truth, and healing, not for who they needed me to be, but for who I was always meant to become.

For most of my life, I didn't realize I was living someone else's version of me. I was taught early on that love looked like sacrifice, that being good meant being quiet, and that my worth depended on how well I could serve others, especially men. My mother, unknowingly passing down her own pain, taught me to please, to put others first, and to equate obedience with value. My father's narcissism painted love as something I had to earn through perfection, silence, and suffering.

At the time, I didn't see it as conditioning. I thought it was just life. I thought it was just *me*.

But as I grew older, I began to feel the weight of living a life that wasn't mine. I was constantly performing, constantly bending, and yet I still felt unseen. Something deep inside me started to whisper:

*This isn't who you are.* That whisper became louder until I couldn't ignore it anymore.

One day, everything I believed about myself cracked. The illusion shattered that I had to earn love, that my voice didn't matter, that I was only as valuable as I was useful. In that breaking, I saw the truth: I had been living in survival, not in self.

It hurt. It shook me. But it also freed me.

That's when I decided to stop carrying the stories that didn't belong to me. I began to dig up the roots, to examine the soil of my childhood, and to understand how it shaped the woman I was becoming. I forgave myself for not knowing sooner. And in that fertile ground, cleared of illusion and watered with truth, I began to plant new seeds.

Seeds of self-love. Boundaries. Joy. Wholeness.

Now, I grow with intention. Not to please, but to live fully. Not to serve blindly, but to stand rooted in who I am. My healing became my rebellion. And my freedom, the garden I'll pass on to the next generation.

Over the course of several months, I immersed myself in relentless research, searching for a way to transform my life into something that truly felt like mine. I was tired of living to please everyone else, constantly carrying the weight of others' happiness on my shoulders, and feeling guilty any time I prioritized myself. I wanted to understand how to break free from those patterns and start showing up for *me*.

Throughout that journey, countless voices guided and inspired me, Bashar's channelings, Dr. Gabor Maté's deep insights on trauma,

Louise Hay's healing affirmations, Jay Shetty's wisdom, Lewis Howes' interviews, Dr. Joe Dispenza's work on rewiring the mind, Steve Bartlett's reflections, and many more. But one key thing I learned along the way was this: I didn't have to accept every word I heard. I only took what truly resonated with me, what felt aligned. The rest was just noise.

For most of my life, my motivation came from my ego, this version of me that I believed I had to be. I chased success, validation, and love, trying to prove my worth through achievement and approval. That persona—the mask I wore—helped me survive in the world, but it wasn't *me*. The awakening stripped that mask away, and for the first time, I saw how much of my life was built around a false identity. For 36 years, I was performing. I didn't even realize it.

Suddenly, I didn't care about being liked, winning, or fitting in. I wasn't trying to play the game anymore because I could finally *see* the game, and that changed everything. My old goals lost their grip on me. They were designed for someone I no longer was. It felt like stepping off a stage and forgetting the script, not because I was lost, but because the role never truly belonged to me.

I hadn't lost motivation. I had simply outgrown the fuel that once drove me. I came to realize I wasn't here to serve my ego, or anyone else's. I was here to *integrate* the ego, to align it with something bigger—my soul. This was the journey of becoming whole again, of moving from fragmentation to unity. And in that place of wholeness, I no longer cared about status or approval. I just wanted to live my truth.

As I moved through my awakening, my mind began to recalibrate. It started rejecting anything fake, forced, or performative. It was liberating and disorienting. I had asked for freedom, but I hadn't realized it would require everything that wasn't real in me to fall away. I entered a kind of limbo, no longer who I was, but not yet who I was becoming. While the world continued rushing by, I found myself sitting in silence, suspended in a kind of psychological pause.

This was the hermit phase, the death before rebirth. A time when I felt nothing, wanted nothing, needed nothing. It was in that stillness that the unconscious finally had space to rise. I was forced to face what I had buried, to feel it, to witness it, to reclaim it. And when I stopped resisting the void, something beautiful began to happen, motivation returned. But it was different now. It wasn't anxious, performative, or tied to some checklist. It felt like remembering not chasing.

This was the emergence of my true self—a quiet inner compass pointing me away from my old life and toward something more honest. As my ego softened and my unconscious integrated, I became capable of living in a place deeper than my personality. Life stopped being about survival and started becoming about *meaning*.

It was beautifully ordinary—guided not by fear of missing out, but by what felt aligned. I no longer chased clarity; I recognized it when it arrived. The inner betrayal I once felt, dragging myself through a life that didn't fit, began to fade. I started to feel pulled by creativity, curiosity, and peace, rather than pushed by pressure or performance. That became my new fuel, trusting my inner guidance to show me the way.

I transformed my ambition into devotion. Not to ego, but to truth. A truth sustained through the soul. I am no longer fragmented. I am now rooted in my wholeness.

How did I do it? How did I find my way back to wholeness? Through my research, I discovered something profound: the path to healing meant returning to my original self, the child within me. Not the baby I once was, but the pure soul that entered the world through the portal of birth, through my mother's womb.

From birth to around age six, a child's brain undergoes rapid development, with evolving brainwave patterns reflecting this growth. In the earliest years (0–2), delta waves dominate, these slow brainwaves are linked to deep sleep and form the foundation for basic brain functions during intense growth. Then, from about ages 2 to 6, theta waves become more prominent. These waves represent a dreamlike, highly receptive state characterized by imagination, creativity, and emotional learning.

During this early childhood phase, children absorb everything around them deeply, building the groundwork for language, memory, and symbolic thinking. Essentially, young children are like sponges, soaking in all the sights, sounds, and feelings of their environment. This absorption creates the very foundation of who we become.

From around age seven onward, children's brain waves begin to shift toward faster frequencies, particularly alpha and beta waves, which are linked to increased alertness, focused attention, and logical thinking. Alpha waves (8–12 Hz) indicate a calm yet awake state, associated with relaxed focus and readiness to learn, while beta waves (12–30 Hz) take over during active thinking, problem-solving, and conscious mental effort.

This shift mirrors the child's growing cognitive abilities, improved reasoning, language development, and self-control. As the brain matures, these faster brain waves support more complex learning, social interaction, and decision-making, marking a transition from imaginative, receptive states to more analytical and goal-directed thinking.

Simply put, this is when a child starts to think independently, weigh options, and make choices. While early decisions might seem small, choosing an outfit or what to eat, the capacity for independent thought is now emerging. Before this stage, children typically looked to their parents for guidance or accepted what was given without question.

During this phase of development, the child begins building their emerging identity, layering new experiences and choices on the foundation laid by the environment and influences absorbed during the formative years from birth to six.

The experiences a child is exposed to and absorbs between the ages of 0 to 6 play a defining role in shaping the foundation of who they will become. If a child is raised in an environment filled with love, nurture, respect, attention, and care, much like a plant given sunlight, rich soil, water, and consistent tending, they are far more likely to bloom into a well-grounded, emotionally secure individual. This kind of stable foundation allows them to build their identity with fewer complications later in life.

However, balance is essential. On one end of the spectrum, if a child is showered with excessive love and protection without being taught about the challenges and realities of life, they may grow up with an unrealistic expectation of how the world works. This can lead to people-pleasing tendencies, dependence on external validation, and vulnerability to manipulation. Their kind and open-hearted nature, while beautiful, can leave them unguarded in a world that isn't always kind in return.

On the opposite end, a child exposed to trauma, neglect, violence, or emotional rejection in these critical early years is likely to develop a fractured and unstable foundation. Attempting to build a life on this shaky ground often leads to repeated emotional and mental breakdowns as they struggle to carry the weight of adulthood without the inner stability needed to thrive. Over time, this instability can manifest in chronic mental health struggles, physical illness, or even suicidal ideation.

In some cases, these survival adaptations can evolve into narcissistic traits in adulthood, emotional manipulation, gaslighting, apathy, entitlement, and exploitative behaviors, as a way to cope with deep, unmet emotional needs and early emotional neglect.

Ultimately, the key to a balanced and resilient life lies in receiving love, affection, and nurturing in a way that is supportive but not overbearing, while also being gently introduced to the realities of life. A child who learns both the warmth of love and the wisdom of discernment is far more equipped to navigate relationships and challenges with clarity, awareness, and inner strength.

This understanding led me to a pivotal realization: the key to my transformation was in dismantling the very foundation I had tried to build my life. I could no longer ignore that this foundation—

formed in my earliest years—was unstable, cracked, and unreliable. If I continued to build on it, I was bound to repeat the same emotional and mental breakdowns I had already endured. It became clear that I needed to rebuild from the ground up.

But how?

After discovering Dr. Joe Dispenza's work on rewiring the brain, something clicked. I learned that in our earliest years, especially from birth to age two, our brains operate primarily in delta wave states, which are deeply connected to subconscious programming and foundational development. As adults, we only return to this state during deep sleep. That's when I realized that if I wanted to reach and reprogram my subconscious, I needed to work with my brain while it was in this receptive state.

So, I began a nightly practice of listening to positive affirmations as I fell asleep, night after night, for six to twelve months. Slowly, I noticed a shift. Negative thought patterns that once ruled my mind began to surface in manageable ways. I could observe them, understand their roots, and let them go. The affirmations began to take their place, gently but steadily. Each day, I noticed subtle changes in my mindset, my emotions, and the way I responded to life. Positive days began to outnumber the negative ones. My self-awareness grew. My inner dialogue softened.

Alongside this practice, I created daily rituals, smoking a joint, sitting with myself, and having raw, honest conversations with my own soul. I wanted to know myself deeply, the way we strive to know a life partner. We invest so much energy in building loving, trusting relationships with others, yet rarely do we give ourselves the same devotion. I decided to become my own soulmate first.

There's a saying: *As within, so without.* I came to understand this deeply. If I wanted to attract genuine love, respect, kindness, and care from others, I had to first offer those things to myself. Because the truth is, you cannot give to others what you haven't first given to yourself. And what you deny yourself, you won't recognize or sustain in someone else.

For two years straight, I committed to working on myself with unwavering dedication. It became a daily ritual like clockwork. I handled my responsibilities at work, but outside of that, I had very few commitments. My children were teenagers by then, mostly independent and doing their own thing. Sometimes they'd sit with me, but often, I was alone and I loved it. After leaving New Zealand, I intentionally cleared my schedule of social obligations and extracurricular distractions. What I found was a deep joy in doing absolutely nothing but sitting in my garden, reflecting, and talking to myself.

I fell in love with my own company. I genuinely enjoyed being with me. One day it struck me. I'm actually really cool to hang out with. No wonder so many people over the years wanted to stay in touch or be close to me, even when I didn't always feel the same way about them.

There were two reasons for that. First, I've always loved solitude, even as a child. I never enjoyed social obligations, especially the pressure to constantly celebrate things. I'm the kind of person who prefers to move with how I feel, and most of the time, I just don't feel like partying. Second, and more honestly, I now realize that my people-pleasing tendencies meant I was simply tolerating many of those relationships. I didn't actually like those people—I just didn't know how to say no. I often found them emotionally needy in ways that repelled me, and I would silently look forward to their absence.

All my life, I've carried this deep sense that I was meant for something more—something bigger than the chaos I was born into. I've always felt like an old soul passing through a world that didn't quite match my inner truth. What helped me survive was my vision, my perspective, and my ability to see the inner child in everyone, no matter their age. I didn't look at people with judgment or hatred but with understanding. Their behavior often spoke volumes about the pain and trauma they were carrying.

I've always had deep empathy. I never played pretend the way others seemed to, I was direct, honest, and unafraid. Titles and power didn't impress or intimidate me. I treated everyone equally. Sometimes I would even mirror back the behavior of emotionally immature adults, not to provoke, but to hold up a mirror. That kind of honesty didn't always win me popularity, but I didn't care. I wasn't here to be liked, I was on a mission. And the truth is, I *liked* me. Anyone else liking me was a bonus—appreciated, sure, but not essential.

It's like ice cream. A little extra sauce is nice, but too much ruins it, and if there's no sauce at all, I'll still enjoy it just the same.

"The first signs of life are whispers of renewal— delicate sparks that awaken the soul to endless possibility."

# CHAPTER 10:
# THE FIRST SIGNS OF LIFE

When I first decided to change my mindset, I didn't expect overnight miracles. For weeks, months even, it felt like nothing was happening, old doubts crept in, and I questioned if I had planted the right seeds at all. Then one morning, as I caught myself pausing before reacting to a frustrating email, something clicked. Instead of the usual anxiety, I felt a calm curiosity. It was tiny, almost invisible,a small green shoot breaking through hard soil. That quiet moment was my first real sign of life, proof that the new me was starting to grow, one mindful choice at a time.

*"Transformation begins not in giant leaps, but in the quiet, persistent whispers of change that first stir the soul."*

Looking back now, I can clearly see all the moments when I would get instantly triggered—angry, reactive, raising my voice over anything that felt like an inconvenience. At the time, I didn't realize how lost I was in my own mind, and how deeply my upbringing and past relationships had shaped that reactive version of me. I was constantly in an invisible battle, trying to get people to understand me—not because I wanted to be right, but because I genuinely wanted everyone to win. I believed in working together, in building something stronger through unity, but it always felt like no one could truly see my heart or my intentions.

Often, I felt like a human version of Siri or Alexa, only called upon when someone needed help, insight, or a sounding board. People would come to me for answers, logic, and clarity, and I gave freely because I saw things clearly and loved being of service. But time and time again, they'd take my advice and do the opposite, almost as if failing on purpose, just to prove a point or diminish my voice. It felt petty and childish. And still, I kept giving.

The years I spent within my family and early relationships were filled with emotional degradation and cruelty. I could never understand why I was treated with so much coldness, harshness, and even evil when all I ever wanted was to share love, support, and build healthy, mutual relationships. I spent 36 years in confusion, asking myself, *Why am I so kind, so generous, and all people seem to do is take?* Sure, they gave me things, money, gifts, but not the kind of love or care that truly mattered. Rarely did anyone offer their time, their wisdom, or step in to guide me out of the darkness when I needed it most.

Why was I left to suffer alone?

Over time, I began to see the truth: people weren't cruel because of me, they were cruel because of their own pain. My strength became a mirror for their weakness. My ability to bounce back, to keep going, to grow in the face of adversity triggered something in them. It confused them. It threatened them. They couldn't understand why I wasn't broken like they were, so they resented me for it. They wanted to pull me into their suffering because misery loves company. My light unsettled their darkness.

It was as if the unspoken message was: *How dare you be yourself? How dare you shine, when we've dimmed our own light for so long?* I was expected to shrink, to serve, to meet their needs without having any of my own. But I see it all now, and I'm done betraying myself just to make others comfortable in their pain.

For years, I felt like I didn't truly exist in this world. My body was here—moving, functioning—but my soul and mind felt detached like they were floating somewhere far away, trapped in a surreal film I never signed up for. It was as if I had been cast in a role written by other people, and molded to fit their expectations. I was a character on autopilot, a background extra called in when needed but expected to be available at all times, unquestioningly.

My mind, body, and soul were constantly uncomfortable—disconnected—and I couldn't explain why. Still, something deep within me pushed me forward. A quiet, persistent voice told me I needed to figure it out, to figure *myself* out. And I knew I would. I knew nothing could stop me because one thing I had always admired about myself was that I was a doer. My life mottos were simple but powerful: *"Make like Nike and just do it"* and *"Ain't nobody got time for that."* These mantras kept me grounded and focused. They gave me the fuel to dig deep, take action, and avoid wasting time on anything that didn't serve my highest good.

Even in the face of adversity, I refused to be held down. I was a woman on a mission—unstoppable.

As I moved through my healing journey, I began to notice subtle shifts within me. Bit by bit, my awareness expanded. I began to see my environment for what it truly was, and it was absurd. My father's immature behavior, my mother's constant gossip her obsessive need to "fix" things, and her persistent attempts to get me to praise my sisters for their achievements, it all felt forced and hollow. I would feel this discomfort rise every time she encouraged communication between us, even though it was painfully obvious they didn't care to hear from me, nor did I feel any connection when they did speak.

I always sensed that my sisters didn't like me. Especially the eldest, it was undeniable. The middle one hid it better, but I could still feel it. And I hated the fake dynamic we all pretended was real. It was exhausting. Nauseating.

But as I healed, I began to truly *see* things. And even when I couldn't fully recognize the changes happening within me, my family could. They would say they missed the "old me"—the bright, bubbly, high-energy version of myself who lit up every room, uplifted moods, looked polished, and made everything feel lighter.

But that version of me was gone.

Now, I was quiet. Moody. My hair was undone, my face expressionless. And while they saw someone falling apart, I was actually sitting in the darkness, mine and theirs, watching, learning, and trying to finally understand what all of it *really* meant.

I began to notice my mother's constant attempts to make me feel insecure, all disguised as concern for my well-being. Not a single day would pass without her commenting on my weight, my appearance, the acne scars and marks on my face, and even the clothes I wore. She would nitpick every little detail as if to say I wasn't worthy of being around them looking the way I did, and that I had to "fix" myself to earn their acceptance. I caught the disgusted looks on their faces, even when they thought I wasn't watching. That's when it hit me: they counted on me not noticing, so they could sneak in their subtle digs and constant criticism, never enough for them to truly love or accept me.

My mother seemed to take a twisted pleasure in breaking us down just to "fix" us again, and this cycle repeated throughout our entire lives. When my oldest sister was a teenager and a little overweight, my mother mocked her relentlessly. She even made a cruel song about it and asked me and my middle sister to sing along. She claimed it was "for her own good"—that she needed to worry about her weight for her health and to be desirable enough for a man to want her. It was malicious, toxic, and deeply abusive. It left my sister battling body image issues and constantly stressed about her appearance.

I couldn't believe I hadn't seen it before, how truly ugly my mother's heart was beneath her carefully crafted image. She always played the innocent victim of my father's cruelty, pretending to be loving and caring toward us while simultaneously tearing us down. It was psychological and emotional manipulation at its worst, a push and pull of hot and cold that bred uncertainty and dependency. She used affection like a drug to keep us hooked, leaving us desperate for connection while maintaining power over us through fear and confusion. Her tactics made it impossible to understand her true intentions, trapping us in a cycle of doubt and control.

I also began to notice how my sisters constantly minimized and excused our parents' harmful behaviors. They would rationalize the abuse, saying things like, *"If it weren't for what we went through, we wouldn't be as successful or driven as we are today."* It was a coping mechanism—normalizing the pain in order to make sense of it. But in doing so, they tolerated the intolerable.

My mother, unwilling to take accountability or face any emotional discomfort, continued her patterns of abuse by turning us against each other. She would speak negatively about my sisters to me, and I can only assume she did the same about me to them, planting seeds of resentment, jealousy, and distrust. It was a manipulative game designed to pit us against one another, forcing us into competition for her limited affection and approval. This constant triangulation shattered our sense of unity and damaged our self-worth. We were taught, on a subconscious level, that we weren't worthy of kindness or love unless we earned it through suffering.

It's no surprise that all three of us ended up in abusive relationships with men, repeating the dynamic we were conditioned to believe was normal.

My mother's manipulation ran even deeper. She used a tactic known as *"crazy-making"*—convincing me that my completely valid reactions to the abuse were wrong, selfish, dramatic, or even abusive themselves. If I stood up to my father's or sisters' toxic behavior, I was accused of being controlling or unreasonable. I was told they were simply being "authentic," and I was the one with the problem of not accepting them.

Over time, I was bullied into silence. I was shamed for speaking out, made to feel guilty for having boundaries, and slowly convinced that I was the hurtful one. That this was what love looked like. That this was how the family operated. I was manipulated into believing I was powerless, that I shouldn't even try to defend myself, and that walking away from mistreatment was not an option.

Becoming aware of all of this was a profound part of my healing journey. There were moments when the realization would hit me so hard, that I'd burst into uncontrollable tears, sobbing as if a valve had been released and years of suppressed emotion came rushing out all at once. It felt like a pipe deep inside me had finally cracked open.

That's when I recognized something deeply unsettling: I was experiencing Stockholm syndrome. It was a psychological response I had unknowingly developed, a trauma bond where, as the abused, I had naturally formed emotional attachments to my abusers as my parents. It was rooted in survival. Whenever my family or my ex-husband showed even the smallest act of kindness during a traumatic situation, my instinct wasn't caution, it was compassion. I would feel an overwhelming sense of empathy, loyalty, and even affection for them. It didn't make sense logically, but emotionally, it was everything I knew.

As time went on, I found myself rationalizing their behavior. I defended them, even to myself. I felt powerless and isolated on so many levels, and yet I'd say things like, *"They're not bad people— they're just wounded,"* or *"They only act this way because they were hurt too."* I told myself that if I just loved them enough, supported them enough, and showed them enough patience and care, maybe they'd heal. Maybe they'd change. Maybe I could be the one to help them return to the good, kind-hearted people I believed they were deep down.

But in doing so, I abandoned myself.

Grieving was one of the most profound and necessary parts of my healing journey from abuse. It wasn't just about mourning what had happened to me, it was about grieving everything I had lost along the way: trust, innocence, a sense of safety, my identity, and at times, even my self-worth. I moved through the stages of grief, denial, anger, sadness, and eventually acceptance, but not in a straight line. I circled back more than once, revisiting emotions I thought I had already laid to rest.

This kind of grief is complex. It's not just about pain, it's about the confusion of losing connection with people I once loved and trusted, even when those people were the source of my suffering. Allowing myself the space to grieve without judgment became essential. It gave me permission to honor my truth and, slowly, to reclaim my voice, my agency, and my wholeness. Healing, I learned, doesn't come from forgetting, it begins when we make peace with what cannot be changed.

Through that healing process, something unexpected emerged: a deeper awareness. I began to see that the people who hurt me were often shaped by their own unresolved trauma. That doesn't excuse the abuse or erase its impact, but it helped me understand that many abusers were once wounded children themselves, raised in environments where emotional neglect, control, or violence were normalized. In many cases, their need for dominance was a way to mask their own shame and powerlessness.

This realization didn't erase my anger or sadness, but it began to shift the emotional weight I carried. Instead of letting their brokenness define me, I transformed that pain into insight. I stopped carrying their damage as if it were my own. I saw their dysfunction for what it was, and in seeing that clearly, I reclaimed my strength.

I chose not to repeat the cycle.

Yes, hurt people hurt people. But I believe healing people can heal others too. As the saying goes, *"An eye for an eye leaves the whole world blind."* So I chose a different path. I chose to walk away, not to take an eye. That, for me, is where true power and true freedom began.

Choosing not to let the harmful behavior of others poison my soul or drag me down to their level was the greatest decision I've ever made. I've always been determined to stay true to myself and protect the source of my life force, my joy, my peace, my world. No matter what I faced, deep within me, I knew no one could truly control me. If I ever allowed mistreatment, it was only because of the vastness of my heart and the love I hold for myself and others. I understood my vision, and my perspective, and even when many chose to misunderstand me and carry their toxic energy, nothing could break me, and nothing ever will. I am a spiritual warrior, winning the psychological battles others tried to impose on me. That victory is my highest achievement, and I am profoundly proud for never betraying myself for the sake of acceptance. I accept myself fully.

Recognizing my strength through everything I experienced and endured was the first true sign of life for me. I accepted that, although it wasn't my fault I found myself in those situations, it was my responsibility to find my way out. I committed myself to healing and understanding both myself and others, reaching a place where I'm fully grounded in the present, no longer lost in my thoughts, confused, or afraid to truly live. After years of merely surviving, living now means stepping into a space where the constant struggle to endure no longer defines every moment. It's a shift from just existing to embracing a deeper presence, where I can finally breathe freely without fear and uncertainty weighing me down. Survival has become a quiet strength that shapes how I view the world and myself. Life feels fragile yet precious, inspiring a new appreciation for simple joys, genuine connections, and the freedom to dream beyond survival. This journey is about reclaiming hope, rediscovering purpose, and embracing the possibility not just to survive, but to truly thrive. This is my time to shine, for me, and no longer allowing anyone to steal my light.

"Patterns shape the paths we walk, but people hold the power to break or rebuild the stories woven into our lives."

# CHAPTER 11:
# PATTERNS AND PEOPLE

I've always watched people closely, not out of suspicion, but out of curiosity and care. Even as a child, I would sit quietly at the edges of rooms, listening more than speaking, noticing more than most. I could sense shifts in tone, body language, in energy. It wasn't something I was taught, it was something I *was*. I used to think I was just "too sensitive," but I later realized I was actually deeply tuned in.

As I got older and began my healing journey, I started seeing it more clearly: people move in patterns. The way they speak when they're hiding something. The way they disconnect when they feel unworthy. The way they hurt others when they're afraid. These weren't random actions—they were repeated rhythms born from their own pain.

The most powerful shift happened when I saw my *own* patterns, how I would overextend, justify, or absorb blame that wasn't mine. Once I began recognizing those cycles, I finally had the power to break them. Understanding patterns didn't just help me make sense of others, it helped me make peace with myself.

"When you've spent your life feeling everything, you learn to see what most people miss. Patterns don't lie, people just get lost in them. But when you learn to see them clearly, you stop taking everything personally and start choosing differently."

Being deeply sensitive and an empath means feeling the emotions and energies of others so intensely that it sometimes feels overwhelming, like carrying the weight of the world on your heart. Through my spiritual healing journey, I discovered that I am one of the rarest types of empaths known as a Heyoka empath. Unlike typical empaths who absorb emotions quietly, Heyoka empaths are mirrors and challengers, they reflect others' feelings back in unexpected ways, often using humor, paradox, or unconventional actions to help people see their truth and heal. This rare gift means I not only feel deeply but also bring transformation by shaking up old patterns and inviting growth, even if it sometimes feels lonely or misunderstood. Finding this part of myself has given me clarity and purpose, helping me embrace my unique role in the spiritual tapestry.

As a child, I always felt like I was from another world like an alien who didn't quite belong here. Earth never truly felt like home, and I carried an intense longing for a place I couldn't name or find. As I progressed on my healing journey, I discovered the concept of being a starseed, and it resonated deeply within me. To be a Starseed is to feel an unexplainable connection to the stars and the cosmos as if your soul comes from a distant world beyond Earth. It carries ancient wisdom, otherworldly perspectives, and a mission to help humanity evolve and heal. Starseeds often feel out of place here, guided by strong intuition and a pull toward spiritual growth and cosmic knowledge. This identity comes with both challenges and gifts—balancing the demands of earthly life while awakening to a greater cosmic purpose, striving to bring light, love, and transformation to the world. For me, this description perfectly captured how I've felt all my life, the weight of the world on my shoulders, and a sense that I'm meant for something big, something that will help heal the people of the world.

Looking back, I realize that I've always had a natural ability to mirror and challenge people—whether it was family, friends, colleagues, or even bosses. I can still recall the look of surprise on their faces as if silently asking, *"How did she see through that?"* or *"Where does she get the nerve to call this out?"* Even when I was being mistreated or enduring emotional pain, I often walked through life fearlessly, making it look easier than it was. I now see that as part of my strength as a Heyoka empath, deeply intuitive, reflective, and unafraid to disrupt dysfunction with the truth.

One clear example comes from my first nursing job at a small clinic. The team was tiny: one doctor, one receptionist who wore multiple hats, from clinic manager to cleaner and me, the nurse. At first, I didn't realize how much this woman was being exploited. Over time, I noticed she was essentially running the entire clinic while also taking work home, spending up to five unpaid hours every night catching up on tasks.

When I found that out, I asked her, half-jokingly but seriously, "Would you like to come clean my house for free?" She looked at me, confused, and said no, of course not. That opened the door for a conversation. I explained that by working those extra hours for free, she was doing exactly that, giving away her time and energy without compensation. I asked her why she would choose to serve her boss over spending that precious time with her family. That moment planted a seed. She slowly started to see her situation through a new lens.

I supported her in small ways, helping with cleaning tasks at the end of the day, taking out my trash, and vacuuming my office. But one day, I had to leave early and didn't get around to it. The next morning, she called me into her office and asked why I hadn't done my cleaning, as if it were a formal responsibility. I reminded her, calmly, that it wasn't my job to clean. I was just helping her out of kindness. She was stunned. She insisted it was part of my role, but when she checked with the doctor who had hired me, he confirmed I was right. I was hired as a nurse, not a cleaner.

Over the next three years, I watched her slowly wake up to the imbalance and manipulation she had been tolerating. We built a strong friendship through it all. Eventually, she became more assertive and less tolerant of the exploitation, and when I finally left, she soon followed, realizing her worth.

The doctor tried to manipulate me too. Once, he called me out of my office to point out smudges on the wall and casually suggested I clean them. I smiled and said, "Thanks for that completely useless information," then walked away. He clarified, awkwardly, that he meant *I* should clean it. I laughed and replied, "Yeah, no—I'm not the cleaner, and you're not saving money off my back."

Another time, he told me a patient had left something for me in the bathroom. Thinking it was a urine sample, I went in—only to find a drop of blood on the toilet seat. I turned around and said, "Oh no, that's definitely for you." He huffed but cleaned it himself.

Later, during our usual end-of-day chats, I decided to break it down for him in a way even a toddler could understand. I said, "If you hired a contractor to build a deck at your house, and he finished 15 minutes early, would you then ask him to clean your bathroom?" He replied, "Of course not." I said, "Exactly. I'm the contractor. This clinic is your house. Clean your own bathroom."

He was taken aback but humbled. From that moment on, I noticed a shift in the way he treated me. A bit more respect. A little less control.

That job was just one example of how I've consistently reflected others back to themselves, calling out manipulation and power games without losing my own sense of worth. As a Heyoka empath, my gift has always been in seeing clearly what others try to hide and having the courage to speak it out loud. And that gift has helped not only me but the people around me—wake up.

At another clinic, which had competed fiercely with two others to hire me, I was given a brand-new office with shiny new equipment, fresh paint, new carpet, and a large window flooding the room with natural light. A new clinic manager started at the same time, and initially, we got along well—sharing laughs and friendly conversations. But at some point, her attitude shifted, unbeknown to me. I began noticing subtle but pointed remarks revealing her insecurities.

The first time was when the clinic owner visited her office. I jokingly said, "Better get back to work before the boss fires me," looking at the doctor. She quickly snapped, "I'm the boss!" I brushed it off as a strange moment of insecurity. Later, while discussing a patient who needed her assistance, I noticed she was packing up early. She routinely left two hours before the rest of us. When I said, "I won't hold you up, we can talk later, you can go" she sharply replied, "Don't do that." That was another moment of impulsive insecurity. Interestingly, she had also recently pushed the doctor to give her a larger office, kicking out the counselor who originally used that space.

Things escalated when she tried to undermine my clinical decisions. A patient, clearly dramatizing for her husband's attention, allowed me to insert a cannula for an iron infusion. After insertion, the patient screamed loudly, inciting her husband's overprotective defense and escalating to an angry confrontation where he accused me of incompetence and demanded to speak to the manager. The manager seized the chance to apologize to the patient on my behalf without asking me what happened, then booked the patient for a follow-up infusion the next week with a different doctor, claiming that this doctor was an expert as they worked with patients with difficult veins in the oncology department, and despite knowing I wouldn't normally do two infusions in one day due to safety risks. I stayed silent, knowing the outcome would be the same.

When Tuesday came, the same drama unfolded, and the doctor joked about being "incompetent too" in front of the manager. I caught the manager's furious glare and smirked inside.

The final straw came when I asked her three weeks in advance for a day off to attend a business meeting for my side hustle. She yelled "NO!" as if I were a child, claiming another nurse had annual leave then, and the only other nurse was too old to work alone. She also demanded I not speak to that nurse about it. Surprised, I spoke to the other nurse anyway, who assured me she was fine working alone. I told the manager this, explaining that as charge nurse, she could cover and I asked as more of a courtesy as I could easily just call in sick that day. She shouted again, "No, and I told you not to speak to her!"

Realizing that reasoning would be useless, I reported the manager's disrespect and unreasonable behavior to the doctor/owner. He was timid and avoided conflict but listened, agreed, and promised to address it. He later told me it was "sorted" and encouraged me to speak with her again, assuring me I'd get the day off. I had told him she hadn't offered me a chance to compromise, like taking a half-day, and requested he attend as a witness. He declined.

Reluctantly, I spoke with the manager again. She was more pleasant but still unsettled. She claimed I never mentioned a half-day off and would have gladly approved it had I asked. I pointed out she never gave me the chance to discuss it and instead yelled at me like a child. She gaslit me, insisting I was misremembering the events. Shocked, I walked away and reported back to the doctor, demanding he resolve the issue or I'd resign. He relied heavily on me as an advanced prescribing nurse, and patients adored me. A week passed with no resolution, so I called in sick to think it over and then submitted my resignation.

I acted with integrity, returning to complete my four-week notice despite the tension. The doctor was relieved I didn't abandon my post. During my final weeks, the manager's petty behavior worsened, poisoning others against me. One day, after I laughed at a joke, the charge nurse snapped at me to "go to my room," then apologized blaming stress. Another time, the doctor accused me of talking negatively about the manager without asking me, citing rumors.

I ignored the drama, focusing on patients, but at day's end, I emailed the doctor outlining my feelings and stating I would contact the nursing union for advice. I asked if he would agree to cut my notice short as the environment felt unsafe. He agreed, and I left it at that.

This situation highlights not only my ability to recognize when someone is behaving like an immature narcissist trying to assert dominance and control but also my emotional intelligence and self-awareness. I'm able to spot the subtle signs, manipulation, an excessive need for attention, lack of empathy, and attempts to belittle others, all tactics used to maintain a false sense of superiority. This clarity lets me see past their surface charm or aggression and understand that their actions stem from deep insecurity and a desperate hunger for power. With this insight, I can protect my boundaries, avoid getting entangled in their drama, and respond with calm strength rather than emotional reactivity, preserving my peace and integrity.

This awareness led me to discover that I'm also considered a dark empath, a narcissist's worst nightmare. A dark empath shares the deep emotional understanding of a traditional empath but pairs it with a keen insight into human psychology and the darker sides of behavior. This unique blend gives dark empaths a powerful edge: they detect manipulation and emotional games from afar and respond with calculated insight rather than blind compassion. To a narcissist, a dark empath is both a challenge and a threat, because they see through facades, resist control tactics, and maintain firm boundaries. Unlike typical victims, dark empaths don't fall into narcissistic traps easily; instead, they navigate these dynamics with empathy, intuition, and guarded strength often unsettling the narcissist's attempts to dominate or exploit.

Growing up as an observant child in the shadow of a narcissistic parent, and then marrying a narcissist, shaped my early life through constant emotional confusion, self-doubt, and the feeling of never being truly seen. Yet, it was through this deep pain that my awakening began. As I moved through my healing journey, layer by layer, I began to recognize the patterns, the manipulation, and most importantly, my own power. Discovering that I am a dark Heyoka empath, a rare, transformative force who mirrors truth through paradox and emotional insight—was like finally finding the missing piece of who I am. This realization gave me the strength to break free, to set unshakable boundaries, and to turn my wounds into wisdom. What once felt like a life of emotional survival has become a path of purpose, clarity, and inner power. In the most unexpected way, my past pain led me to my greatest awakening.

What I've learned from my journey is a fundamental truth that has helped me move through life fearlessly: every single person, no matter who they are now, was once a child. Beyond my gift of discernment and being a Heyoka empath, my unique perspective is that I see people through the eyes of children. I don't just see adults, I notice the childlike behaviors many adults exhibit but refuse to acknowledge because they won't take responsibility for them like a child would.

I understand how a person's mind works because you can't reason or argue with a child in an adult's body, what you'll get instead is deflection, blame-shifting, and avoidance, just as a child might do with a sibling. Many adults are emotionally stunted, stuck in their childlike mindset, and so they behave accordingly. And when there are many people like this, others often respond in kind, like children reacting to being bullied by another child.

Children can be surprisingly skilled manipulators. Their natural innocence and charm often mask a deep instinct to survive, seek attention, or gain control in a world that feels overwhelming. They test boundaries, play adults against each other, and use emotional tactics like guilt, tantrums, or pleading, not out of malice, but from a basic need to get their needs met. Since children are still learning emotions and social dynamics, their manipulation can be subtle and persistent, making it difficult for caregivers to set boundaries without feeling torn. Understanding this helps us respond with patience and clear guidance, teaching healthier ways to communicate and express needs.

Adults who remain emotionally stuck in their childlike state often carry these survival tactics especially manipulation, into their grown-up lives. Because they never fully developed emotional maturity or healthy coping skills, they rely on guilt-tripping, blame-shifting, or attention-seeking to avoid vulnerability or get what they want. These patterns become deeply ingrained, causing struggles with true connection, empathy, and responsibility. Instead of healing their wounds, they use manipulation to control others, seeking safety or importance. This arrested emotional growth traps them in cycles of conflict and isolation, damaging relationships and blocking genuine fulfillment.

That's why teaching emotional intelligence is so vital. It gives people the tools to understand, manage, and express their emotions in healthy ways, building stronger relationships and wiser decisions. Emotional intelligence helps individuals face life's challenges with resilience and empathy, easing conflicts and improving communication. When people learn to recognize their own feelings and those of others, they become more compassionate, self-aware, and adaptable—qualities that foster personal well-being and create more supportive communities. Ultimately, nurturing emotional intelligence lays the groundwork for healthier mental health, greater social harmony, and a more emotionally balanced world.

"I moved through the shadows of borrowed love, where strings pulled hearts and silence grew thick. Through the thorns of narcissism and the hush of hidden wounds, I bled, I broke, I bloomed. And in the stillness beyond survival, I met myself—wild, radiant, and finally free."